forget me not

from the life of WILLA HAVISHAM

COLEEN MURTAGH PARATORE

SCHOLASTIC PRESS / NEW YORK

Library of Congress Cataloging-in-Publication Data

Paratore, Coleen, 1958-
   Forget me not : from the life of Willa Havisham / by Coleen Murtagh Paratore. — 1st ed.
      p. cm.
Summary: During a Cape Cod summer, Willa is enjoying her relationship with "JFK" Kennelly and the challenges of planning a wedding all by herself, but when jealousy enters her love life, best friend Tina pulls away, and the bride proves impossible to please, a sweet dog begins to turn things around.
   [1. Dating (Social customs) — Fiction. 2. Friendship — Fiction. 3. Weddings — Fiction. 4. Mothers and daughters — Fiction. 5. Dogs — Fiction. 6. Cape Cod (Mass.) — Fiction.] I. Title.
   PZ7.P2137For 2009
   [Fic] — dc22
                                  2008040712

ISBN-13: 978-0-545-09401-6
ISBN-10: 0-545-09401-1

10 9 8 7 6 5 4 3 2 1   09 10 11 12 13 14

Printed in the U.S.A.   23
First edition, May 2009

The text type was set in Sabon.
Book design by Lillie Mear

To my "most fun" friend,
Kathy Johnson
—C.M.P.

Contents

CHAPTER 1

Sea-Spired

I wiped away the weeds and foam,
I fetched my sea-born treasures home;
But the poor, unsightly, noisome things
Had left their beauty on the shore,
With the sun and the sand and the wild uproar.
— Ralph Waldo Emerson

I open my journal and begin to write:

You must be brave to walk the beach alone. After all, you are only human. You may be simply looking for heart-shaped rocks or orange jingle shells, when, in a blink, three giants — Air, Water, and Earth — might converge upon you to form Fire. Fired, inspired, sea-spired, your heart speaks a language only you can hear.

Suddenly, your problem is solved, your path is clear, you have a wonderful idea! Lighter now, happier, your pace quickens as you turn home. The footprints you made only minutes ago are now part of the infinite sea.

A new you makes new prints in the sand, new marks upon the planet, dinosaur-size next to the birds — the seagulls, terns, and plovers.

The beach is never the same beach twice.

Blink, and it changes.

Blink, and it changes.

Blink, and you are changed.

I stop writing, read it over, smile. *Such grand thoughts by the sea, Willa.*

I ruffle through my beach bag for a water bottle. No luck. How could I have forgotten one? We have a whole fridge full at home. My mother ordered a hundred cases with our new green-and-gold inn logo: "Only the best for Bramblebriar guests. Fresh from a mountain stream."

It's eight-thirty A.M. I still have some time before work. Leaving my bag, I walk out along the Spit, a long narrow stretch of beach with calm Popponesset Bay on one side, the wide open Atlantic Ocean on the other. It's my favorite place in the world.

Three tiny birds, piping plovers they're called — white bellied, mottled brown-and-tan feathers, stick legs, just inches high — scurry along in front of me, peck, peck, pecking for breakfast crabs. *Good morning, Plovers.*

When I reach the prettiest part of the Spit, there are workers hammering wooden stakes into the sand, stringing red ropes between them. They look over at me and I wave. Every summer about this time, the Massachusetts Audubon Society cordons off sections of the beach where the piping plovers and the terns, two types of endangered birds, are nesting. This year they're closing off an unusually large area of grade-A top-choice Bramble beach. People aren't going to like this at all.

Right now, the Spit is just sand and birds. By noon, the boats will have landed and anchored and the beach will be covered with blankets, umbrellas, tables and chairs, grills, coolers, volleyball nets, toys, and tons of people. Come Fourth of July, you won't be able to walk without stepping on somebody's sand castle.

Every summer there's always a bit of local nastiness about the endangered bird thing because you can't bring dogs on the beach when the birds are nesting. Dogs might trample the birds' fragile eggs. Seagulls launch sinister aerial attacks, but you can't put a leash on a seagull. Some people ignore the rules and let their dogs run free. Other people call the hotline to snitch.

It makes the papers for a day or two and then *poof*; it's over until next year. I don't pay too much attention. We don't have a dog. My mother says we aren't "dog people."

But this year the birds aren't just messing with dog-people fun. This summer, they're messing with boat-people fun. Judging from the size of the roped-off area, there's an extra-big batch of baby birds on their way. Those fancy yacht owners will be batty about birds taking over their favorite part of the beach. This could get interesting.

At the tip of the Spit I stop and head back the way I came. My throat is tight and achy now. I can't believe I forgot water. The waves lap loudly, taunting me. Water as far as my eyes can see. *"Water, water, every where, nor any drop to . . ."*

"Willa!" My new friend, Mariel Sanchez, is coming up over the dune. Dripping wet, out of breath, she hurries toward me, carrying something. Mare is an early-bird beach girl, too. I walk; she swims, way far out by the buoys. I would never swim out that far.

"Look what the tide brought in," Mare says.

It's a black rubber snorkel with goggles attached, all tangled up in slimy seaweed.

"That's cool, Mare."

"I've always wanted to snorkel," she says, her brown eyes glistening.

"And look, Willa, these are *new*." Mare strips away the straggly green grass. "At first, I thought maybe I should leave them here . . . the owner would come looking. But then I saw this."

She points to the brand name on the snorkel. *Mares*.

"My name's right on it!" she says, laughing. "It's obviously a gift for me!"

I smile.

Mariel blows into the snorkel to clear the airway, then wipes out the eye sockets on the goggles and adjusts them over her face. "See ya, Willa!"

Seconds later, hip-level in the water, Mariel leans face forward and she's off.

"Bye," I shout. "Be careful."

That girl is so free, she amazes me. No worries about where the snorkel came from, or germs, or how she doesn't have flippers, or anything. Mariel Sanchez gets an idea and swims with it.

When I first met Mare earlier this year, I didn't like her at all. She wanted the same part I wanted in the Bramble town play: Emily in *Our Town*. She got the part. Then I thought she was after my boyfriend JFK's heart. It seemed she was ruining my life.

I was wrong. We're getting closer now. We have a lot in common. We both love books and the beach.

I walk faster, thirstier. When I reach my bag, I fling it over my shoulder and slip on my comfy Swiss cheese sandals, smiling at the sunflower buttons I stuck in yesterday. All my friends are wearing these shoes, decorated differently to make them unique.

As I trudge up the old gray wind-weathered stairs, everyone else is coming down. It's a perfect beach day, but I'm on lunch duty. We run the Bramblebriar Inn in town and this is our busiest season. That's the thing about a family business; the whole family helps. And we're a small family — just me, Mom, and my new stepfather, Sam, whom I just started calling "Dad."

At the top of the stairs, my best friend, Tina Belle, and my barely tolerable friend, Ruby Sivler, are getting out of the Sivlers' car. Ruby's mother toots as she zooms off, their fluffy dog, Pookie, in the passenger seat with goggles on like the Red Baron.

Tina and Ruby are wearing bikini tops with matching orange-and-pink flowered sarongs wrapped low on their hips. They look like models on a photo shoot, like sophomores in college, not the sophomores in high school we'll be this fall. Tina flings back her long blond hair and adjusts her silver hoop earrings. Ruby flings back her long red hair, diamond belly ring sparkling in the sun. Tina says something and they squeal, laughing. Two boys watch, mesmerized. The one in the Red Sox cap holds out his cell phone and shouts. Tina and Ruby wave like mermaids, hamming it up for the camera.

When Tina sees me, she acts awkward. "Willa . . . hi. Where you going?"

"Home. I have to work."

Ruby's lip snivels at the sound of that horrible "w" word. "Work" is not something a Sivler girl does. You pay people to do that sort of thing.

"Oh, don't go, Willa," Tina says, clutching my arm.

I feel a little less jealous now.

Ruby lowers her designer sunglasses and squints past me like, "Willa, move; you're clouding my view."

"Don't you remember?" Tina says. "Today's the day. The last Saturday in June. *They're coming at ten!*"

"Who's coming at ten?"

Tina and Ruby look at each other, shaking their heads in disbelief. They lean toward me and whisper-shout: *"The lifeguards!"*

"Oh, right." How could I forget?

Today's the day the college student lifeguards officially ascend their thrones. One bronzed, buff, and beautiful prince-of-a-boy will rule from each tall gray chair. Most beaches have boy and *girl* lifeguards, of course, but at Sandy Beach it's all boys. The lady who hires the lifeguards has three sons and they get jobs for their friends. It's a monopoly or a dynasty or some "ee" or other. All I know is that someone is handling auditions, because I've never seen a goober yet. Every single one is hot. Tina and I used to climb the dunes with our binoculars to spy, wondering what their names were, dreaming of the day we'd be old enough to date them. We're still not old enough.

Besides, I already have a boyfriend, my own age. I touch the silver heart locket around my neck. Joseph Frances Kennelly, "JFK," gave it to me. We have a date later.

Ruby stares at the locket. "Oh, that's right, Willa, we forgot. You're married. We understand, don't we, Tina? We won't tempt you. Will we?"

We. We. Each "we" stings like a jellyfish. *I hate you, Ruby Sivler. Tina and I are the "we." You're the annoying third.* Or at least that's how it's always been.

Ruby grabs Tina's arm and pulls. "Come on, Teen, let's get a good spot."

Teen?

Tina looks at me. Her eyes are sad. I can tell she's torn. I'm torn, too. *BFF. Best friends forever.* How many times have we written that? Ever since I moved here to Cape Cod, we've been tight as twins. But before I came, Tina and Ruby were best friends. They have a lot in common. Lately, it seems even more so.

"Call me later, Willa," Tina says.

"Yeah, sure," I say.

Biking home, the tears come. I don't want to lose my best friend. Why do I have to go to work? Why can't I just enjoy my summer like everybody else?

At the stone fence in front of our inn, I see a paper taped on the Bramble Board. It's where we post happy quotes and town events. When I get closer, I see that on the paper there is a crudely drawn bird inside a red circle, with a diagonal slash line through it and, in messy handwriting across the bottom, the words: "We serve plovers piping hot with fries."

That's awful. I yank the paper off and look around. *Who would do such a thing?*

I bound up the stairs, past two guests playing checkers in the lobby, and into the kitchen for a water bottle. I chug it down and toss it into the recycling bin. *Ahhh.*

"Willa!" my stepfather, Sam, shouts, coming in from the garden.

Good, I want to show him this paper. But then I see his face. Usually a Buddha-like pillar of peaceful, Sam looks manic as a monkey. He drops a wicker basket of green beans on the counter, spilling them everywhere. He wipes sweat from his forehead, leaving a dirty rainbow. "Willa, I need your help."

"Sure, Dad, anything." My heart is pounding. I've never seen Sam so wired.

"Aunt Ruthie's coming. And she wants to get married. Here. Next week. Your mother says that's crazy, 'It just can't be done,' and so I'm begging you. Can you do it? Can you possibly plan a wedding in a week?"

I burst out laughing, relieved. Then Sam does, too.

"Sure," I say. "No problem. They don't call me the wedding planner's daughter for nothing. But I have one very, very crucial question."

"Of course, Willa, what?"

"Who the heck is Aunt Ruthie?"

CHAPTER 2

"Greenzilla"

What is a weed?
A plant whose virtues have not yet been discovered.
— Ralph Waldo Emerson

Ruthie is Sam's big sister. He hasn't seen her in years. An old neighbor sent Ruthie one of the bride magazine articles about the weddings we do at the Bramblebriar Inn, and Ruthie wrote Sam to ask if she could get married here. She's on her way home from South America right now. Ruthie works for Planet Partners, an organization that helps bring safe drinking water to impoverished areas around the world.

"Ruthie's skinny as a string bean," Sam says, holding up a bean to illustrate his point, "but she'll wallop you like a watermelon." He pounds his fist in his palm. "She's absolutely possessed about saving the planet. Preserving waterfalls, the wilderness, the whip-poor-wills and wallabies, wildflowers . . . *weeds*."

"What's wrong with that?" I pick beans up off the floor and toss the basket into the sink, turning on the water to rinse them off. "We care about the planet, too. We recycle and compost and . . ."

"You don't understand," Sam says. "Ruthie is a fanatic. Our mother used to call her 'Ruthie the Ruthless.' She's like some evil environmental super-hero. All she needs is a green cape. My sister won't stop until she single-handedly saves the planet, never mind how many people she plunders in the process."

"Sam . . . Dad, come on," I say, spraying water over the beans, rinsing off the garden dirt. I try not to laugh. "Aren't you stretching the taffy a bit?"

"No, Willa, I'm not. I still have mental scars from high school. Ruthie would stand outside the bathroom with a stopwatch, timing me when I took a shower. If I exceeded my quota, she'd bang on the door scream-ing, 'Do you know how many gallons of water you wasted, Sam? Do you? Do you know how many people will die from thirst today, Sam, while YOU are wast-ing precious, potable water? DO YOU KNOW HOW MANY? Do you, Sam?' My friends used to call ahead of time to make sure Ruthie wasn't home before they came over. Once, I was eating a ham sandwich with my girlfriend Becky, and Ruthie lunged at us in the kitchen, sobbing: 'How can you eat something that had eyes! *Eyes!* Two of them. Probably brown ones just like you, Becky.'

"Becky lost her appetite. Me, I lost Becky."

I burst out laughing.

"*Willa*," Sam says. "This is serious. Ruthie's not human. She's a lean-green-mean-menacing-ma . . ."

"Sam!" I shut off the water, dry my hands off quickly on a towel. I walk over, rest my palm on Sam's shoulder, and look into his eyes. "It's okay, Dad. Settle down. Take a deep breath." I model breathing. "There you go. In, out, in, out. That's right. Good."

Sam seems to calm down a bit.

"So Aunt Ruthie's a *Greenzilla*? Piece a cake. I've watched Mom handle Bridezillas for years. I've got the Stella skills. You'll see."

I can't wait to meet this lady. This is gonna be a blast!

"You don't understand," Sam says. "Your mother and Ruthie are complete opposites, North and South Pole opposites. They'll drive each other crazy. Your mother's a neat freak; Ruthie's a slob. Stella likes rules and order. Ruthie likes Reiki and oracle readings. Just wait till you see her moon salutations."

Oh, my gosh, this is going to be great. Wait till I tell Tina!

"But . . ." Sam takes another good, deep, cleansing

breath. "She *is* my only sister." He's calmer now, his good old Sam-the-man reason returning. "And she's not expecting anything *big* for her wedding." He pulls a folded-up letter out of his shirt pocket and looks it over. "It's just going to be Ruthie and her fiancé, Spruce, and a few close friends."

"His name is Spruce?"

"Yes," Sam says, smiling, "but, who knows, he might be a great guy. They're headed off to Washington right after the wedding for the Greenvolution March on the Fourth of July. Ruthie says she'd like the wedding outdoors, nothing fancy. It just has to be strictly eco-friendly, with no animals injured in the process and —"

My mother comes in. Sam stops talking. We're both extra-sensitive around her these days. Mom had a miscarriage last month, and we all feel horrible, but nobody's supposed to talk about it. I feel bad for my mother, and for Sam, and me — I was excited about having a baby sister or brother — but it's a silent subject. Sam, Nana . . . we've all been extra-specially considerate, but my mother deals with pain by building ice barge barricades around herself. I try, but sometimes it's hard to be nice to ice.

"Willa, please check the vases on the tables before

lunch," she says. "Be sure they have fresh water. And I don't want any deadheads on the dahlias."

"Sure, Mom," I say. I lower my voice. "Don't worry, Dad. Give me the letter. I'll come up with a plan. Oh, and, wait, I have something to show you."

I hand Sam the nasty paper about the piping plovers. He reads it and frowns.

"I'll look into this," Sam says. "This I can handle. Fair-trade barter, okay?"

"What?"

"Ruthie will explain the concept to you. She won't expect to pay a cent for the wedding. She'll offer some sort of service in exchange. Do our star readings or . . ."

Oh, my gosh. This is going to be great.

"Okay, so a fair trade of worries, then?" I say to Sam. "You tackle the plover pirates. I'll tackle Ruthie the Ruthless. Deal?"

"Deal."

"Done."

CHAPTER 3

Sweet Rosie Sweets

*A friend may well be reckoned the masterpiece
of nature.*

— Ralph Waldo Emerson

It's nearly three when we finish clearing the lunch trays from the sunporch. "Everyone raved about the triple-berry shortcake," I tell my friend Rosie, our baker and assistant head chef.

"Thank you, Willa," Rosie says quietly. She steals a glance at my mother, who is sitting at the table doing paperwork. "But you can't really miss with fresh berries in season."

"Don't be modest, Rosie," I say, stacking plates in the dishwasher. "You are *soooo* talented. That shortcake was sublime."

I look quickly at my mother. As expected, she rolls her eyes about "sublime." What's the use of cool words if you can't show them off now and then?

"And what was that spice in the shortcake, Rosie? It was familiar, but I couldn't say for sure."

Rosie smiles.

"Everybody was just buzzing about dessert, Rosie," I continue. "That big family reunion group from New Jersey, the Moscatellos, asked if it could be on the menu again tonight, and the Red Hat ladies from Rhode Island wondered if you'd please share the recipe for the cookbook they're writing."

"They're writing a cookbook?" Rosie says.

"Yes," I say. "It's called *Red Hot Hats in the Kitchen*."

My mother clears her throat and looks at the clock. I know Stella's thinking, *Let's hurry up; it's nearly time to start the soups and sides for dinner.*

"You know what, Rosie?" I say. "I think you should write a cookbook about desserts. Nobody does sweets like you. And my grandmother knows publishers. Sales people from publishing companies call on her at Sweet Bramble Books. You could do a whole series. A pie book, a cake book, a cookie book. And you should have your own TV show, too. You could call it *Rosie's Sweets* ... or *Sweet Rosie Sweets* ... or *Rosie, Sweet and Simple*."

My mother sighs loudly.

Rosie laughs and shakes her head. "Willa, enough."

"That's right, Willa, enough," my mother says. "You're embarrassing Rosie."

Even though the *Cape Cod Times* wedding supplement called the Bramblebriar Inn signature wedding cake that Rosie created the "crème de la crème wedding cake to copy this season," and our good family friend Chickles Blazer of the Blazer Buick fortune — we hosted her daughter Suzanna Jubilee's wedding here last month — says it's the best cake she's ever tasted (and, trust me, Mama Blazer has sampled her fair share of frosting), Rosie continues to be absolutely mousemodest about her confectionery genius.

I cut myself a second helping of shortcake. *Mmmm, yum.* Rosie plops another dollop of whipped cream on top. "Nutmeg," she whispers, and winks at me.

My mother stands up with some envelopes in her hand. "Would you drop these off at the post office on your way home, Rosie?"

"Sure thing, Stella."

I walk outside with Rosie. I ask her if she'll make a cake for Ruthie Gracemore's wedding next Saturday night and help me plan the dinner, too.

"No problem, Willa," Rosie says. "Just tell Stella

to put me on the schedule that night. I'll oversee the kitchen."

"But you're working the Caldor wedding all Saturday afternoon," I say. "You'll be exhausted."

"Don't worry about me, Willa. I'm a big girl. I want things to be just right for Sam's sister's wedding. Your father is such a good man. I'd do anything to help him out, and *you*. Besides, I sure could use the money."

When I go back inside the kitchen, Stella is waiting for me with her arms folded across her chest. "Willa, I would appreciate it if you didn't actively try to get our employees to leave us. It's hard enough finding good help on the Cape without —"

"Is that how you think of Rosie, Mom? As 'help'? Rosie is our friend."

My mother huffs. "There's nothing derogatory about the term 'help,' Willa. We have several workers we count on. Rosie, Darryl, Makita . . . we couldn't run this place without them . . . and Betty and Mae-Alice, the housekeeping staff . . . and the laundry girls."

"The laundry girls?"

"You know who I mean, the girls who wash the linens. We've got thirty rooms in the inn, plus all the cottages, six clean bath towels in each room every day, and then there's the sheets, pillowcases, table-cloths, and napkins. . . ."

"Don't the laundry girls have names?"

"Oh, Willa, please, they're part-timers. Mae-Alice hires them. I cut their checks. Simple as that. This is a business."

"But this is our home, too. Rosie is like a sister to me. Maybe we won't be so close to everyone, but we should at least know the names of the people who work here."

"Fine," my mother says, standing up abruptly.

When Stella Havisham is done, she's done. There's never a question who's boss. She didn't earn her MBA in a beauty pageant, although she could win any beauty contest she entered. My mother is stunning. Sleek black hair, jade-green eyes, peach-perfect skin. And she knows how to run a business. My mother ran one of New England's most successful wedding planning businesses. Now she runs one of the hottest inns on Cape Cod and we host weddings here.

When I was younger, Stella wouldn't let me anywhere near her wedding planning studio. She was worried I would grow up with my head in the clouds, waiting for Prince Charming, instead of working hard in school. But she finally realized she doesn't have to worry about me. I've got my sights set straight on college. And so, just this past year, she let me assist her with the weddings. We did two weddings together for good friends last month. Suzanna Blazer, whose mother I mentioned before, and our town minister, Sulamina Mum. I was maid of honor in both! It was a magical month.

My mother huffs and crosses her arms again. "Why don't you come to the next staff meeting, Willa, and we'll have everybody introduce themselves."

"Fine, Mother. I will," I huff back and cross my arms. "Oh, and, Sam said he talked to you about his sister, Ruthie, wanting to get married here next Saturday. I know we have the Caldor-Hollister wedding at eleven with the reception on the lawn at one, but if I plan Ruthie and Spruce's wedding for that night, say around six out in the Labyrinth, would that be okay?"

"His name is *Spruce?*" My mother rolls her eyes. "Oh pa-lease. What is he, a pine tree? I heard Ruthie's a tree hugger, but . . ."

"I know, Mom, but, *come on,* she is Sam's only sister and we've never even met her."

Mom sighs. "I told Sam that planning a wedding in a week was out of the question. We have a booking earlier that day and Katie Caldor must have my complete attention all —"

"Mom, listen. What if I take care of everything, every detail of Aunt Ruthie's wedding, so you won't even have to think about it? Would that be okay?"

We hear loud laughter outside and turn toward the window. My mother smiles and then looks sad, watching two of the Red Hats riding up and down on the new seesaw Sam put in last month. Sam set up swings and a sandbox, too. He said it was for younger guests at the inn, but I think he had the baby in mind. Poor Sam. Poor Mom. I hope maybe they'll try again.

"Come on, Mom. Let me plan the wedding. Family is important. Aunt Ruthie is Sam's only sister, after all."

"Okay, Willa, enough with the guilt." Mom shakes her head and frowns. Then her eyes meet mine and I smile. Her face brightens and she smiles, too.

"As always, Willa, your heart is in the right place. And I appreciate your enthusiasm. And it is summer vacation and you did do such a lovely job helping me plan the weddings last month. I'd say you've passed your apprenticeship with flying colors."

"Thanks, Mom," I say, beaming. My mother's never one to pile on the praise.

Stella looks out through the open door. A breeze ruffles her hair. She smiles, watching a Red Hat climb up the sliding board. "Okay, Willa. Go ahead. You have my blessing. We'll consider this your solo wedding planning debut."

Whoo-hoo! "Thanks, Mom!" I hug her.

My first wedding. Whoo-hoo!

Just wait until Tina hears. Willa the Wedding Planner.

CHAPTER 4

Wild Rhymes

*'Tis the good reader that makes the good book; . . .
in every book he finds passages which seem
    confidences or asides
hidden from all else and unmistakably meant for his ear.*
— Ralph Waldo Emerson

I head up to my room, exhausted. Good time for a catnap, not that we have cats, just the barn cats that roam the fields. Real pets would be way too messy for my mother. Stella likes things squeaky-clean. Paw prints on a Persian carpet or cat hairs on a white wing-back chair would drive her batty. When I need a pet fix, I go to Nana's and hang out with her scrappy dog, Scamp, and his sister, Muffles, a big, old, fluffy gray cat who loves the sunny window ledge at Sweet Bramble Books.

Tired from my walk and work, I hit the pillow.

An hour later, I wake up. I reach for a book, *Green Angel*, by Alice Hoffman. It's a short book and I only have a few pages left. I'm trying to read a book a day until the end of July. I asked Mrs. Saperstone, my librarian friend, to suggest some short but powerful books — I'm calling them "skinny-punch books" — then I asked Nana to order them for me in paperback. I like having my own copies of books so I can read them with a pen in my hand, marking things that move me. I write the date on the inside front cover when I finish reading it, so that when I look back someday, I can see what I was thinking about and feeling then. Sam taught me that trick. Sam is an English teacher by profession. Now he helps run the inn — he's our main chef — but I liked when Sam was our substitute teacher last semester when Dr. Swaminathan was in India.

Yesterday, I read *Bronx Masquerade* by Nikki Grimes. It's about a bunch of kids who sort out big issues in their lives by writing poetry, which they read aloud at school every Friday. I can't wait to tell JFK about it. He likes writing rhymes.

I open the drawer of my nightstand and take out my trusty bag of saltwater taffy, unwrap a lemon-lime, "lemmego-lime" Nana calls it, and pop it in. *Mmmm, yum.*

I mark many pages of *Green Angel*, underlining beautiful images, writing "nice," "yes," and "love that" in the margins. In the story, fifteen-year-old "Green" is learning to heal and find hope after losing her family in a disaster. In the end, she decides she will tell their stories:

> *"Every white page looked like a garden, in which*
>   *anything might grow.*
> *I sat down at the table with the pen and ink. I*
>   *spread out the clean, white pages.*
> *Then and there, I began to tell their story."*

So lovely, so hopeful. This is definitely going on my "Willa's Pix" list of recommended books.

I look at the clock. Almost time to get ready for my date with JFK. I pick up the book on Emerson that Sam bought for me. Ralph Waldo Emerson was a famous nineteenth-century American poet and essayist. I first discovered this book in Sam's study upstairs and when Sam noticed how interested I was, he ordered me my own copy. Sam knows I like to read with a pen in my hand, marking it up, making the book my own. Sam says I read like a writer.

To me reading and writing are inseparably connected. Someday I want to write books. My wonderful Gramp Tweed, whom I loved so much, told me he thought I'd be a writer. Gramp said the best way to prepare for that was to read all the best books I could. That was very good advice.

Emerson kept a journal just like I do. On June 27, 1839, he wrote:

> "*I wish to write such rhymes as shall not suggest a restraint,*
> *but contrariwise the wildest freedom.*"

The wildest freedom, nice. I like that. I wonder if JFK has written any new rhymes? He writes rap lyrics, good ones, about important things. JFK says rap is like poetry, but it's music. I look at the clock. He'll be here soon. He wouldn't tell me where we're going, but he's awfully excited about it. He said he wanted to surprise me.

I shower and get dressed, pull on a pink T-shirt and my favorite jean shorts. I put on some makeup, towel dry my hair, scrunching up curls on one side, combing straight the other, my signature hairstyle, "the Willa." Ruby Sivler actually invented it for me. At least there's that one nice thing between us. I think about Tina and Ruby hanging out together, checking out the lifeguards at the beach, and then I push that thought from my mind.

I pick up my locket, open the heart, and smile at the faces, JFK on one side, me on the other. I snap the heart shut and clasp the chain around my neck.

JFK is waiting for me at the kitchen door like I asked. That way we won't have to make chitchat with the guests on the front porch. The Red Hats got one look at my guy last night and were all so absolutely smitten, they nearly locked him up in the library so they could talk to him.

JFK was a good sport. He's always such a good sport.

But today I'm being selfish. I want my boyfriend all to myself.

JFK is wearing long tan shorts and a yellow polo shirt. His brown hair is streaked lighter from the summer sun, nearly collar length and wavy.

"Ready?" He smiles with those sea-blue eyes I could sail to Singapore in.

"Ready," I say.

Chef Sam looks over at us from the stove. "Have a good time," he says.

"Thanks, Mr. Gracemore," JFK says.

"Bye, Dad. See ya later."

"Where are we going anyway?" I ask JFK. "You've had me wondering all day."

"You'll see," he says, smiling. "You won't be disappointed. But bring a jacket. It could get chilly."

We take our bikes. It's still gorgeous out. I love these long summer days.

Passing through town, I see Nana's store, Sweet Bramble Books, a combination bookstore and candy shop, is bustling busy. We love the tourists. In July and August, Bramble balloons to three times its normal size with summer visitors. Small stores like Nana's depend on that business.

Biking side by side, I tell JFK about Emerson, the part about rhymes and freedom. "How's your writing coming?" I ask.

"It was flowing today," he says. "I was mowing the lawn, mindless, and then all of a sudden, over the roar, I started getting more lines about the war. Hey, that rhymes." He smiles. "Flags can't hide the body bags. Had enough talk. Time to walk. People dying. Stop the lying. Don't see *your* kids on the line fighting. Made in America."

"Whoa," I say. "Powerful."

"What about you?" he says. "Writing any more letters to stir up trouble?"

He means the letter I wrote to the *Cape Times* about the lack of affordable housing on Cape Cod. A wealthy couple from New Seabury read my letter and started a foundation to build houses for low-income residents.

"No, just my journal."

JFK leads us toward Sandy Beach, way down at the far end. When we come up over the hill, we leave our bikes in the rack, stepping around the cinnamon-sweet smelling *rugosa*, beach roses. JFK takes my hand. "Guessed the surprise yet?"

"No," I say. "I haven't got a clue."

He squeezes my hand. "Wait till you see."

At the top of the stairs he stops and points. "There she is, by the jetty." His face is shining like a kid at the gummy fish bin in Nana's store. "Isn't she beautiful?"

I look down.

No, it can't be.

It is.

A boat.

A very small sailboat next to that very big sea.

The sail is red-and-white striped, with a black fish on the top.

I gulp. Oh, no. I can't.

No way can I go sailing.

CHAPTER 5

Sailing Lessons

Every sweet hath its sour.

— Ralph Waldo Emerson

"What's the matter, Willa?" JFK is staring at me. "You look scared."

I look at him. He looks disappointed.

"No, I'm fine," I say, "just surprised, that's all." Images of the boat tipping, me sinking, are filling my mind. "Wow, this is great. Awesome."

"Come on," JFK says, starting down the stairs, all excited again.

I follow, feeling seasick inside. *Just tell him, Willa, he'll understand. No, you'll spoil it for him. Look how happy he is!*

"I've been saving for a boat," JFK says, "but I was still a couple hundred dollars short. Then my parents pulled this out of the hat. They saw my report card and went squirrelly. Straight As, but

don't tell anybody. I don't want to spoil my image."
He winks at me and smiles with that dimple to
die for.

*Don't think about dying, Willa. Nothing will bite
you. You will not drown.*

"And, get this," JFK says. "They said if I pull
straight As again next year, they'll buy me a used car
for my sixteenth birthday. Sweet, huh?"

"Nice bribe," I say.

"You're not kidding," JFK says. "That's what thinking about college will do to otherwise sane and
normal penny-pinching parents. I watched the process with my big sister, Kerry. They would have done
anything to help her get into Skidmore. She had her
heart set on that school, and Saratoga's a really cool
place."

"Yes, I went there with Tina on vacation one summer. Saw the racetrack and the ballet. Do you think
you want to go to college there, too?"

"Me? No, I've been planning on Boston College
since I was in fourth grade. My teacher, Miss Spooner,
went there. I had a crush on her. Every boy in the
school did. Besides, my dad went to BC and my grandfather, too, but these days it's almost impossible to
get in. You've got to have great grades, ace the SATs,

be a star athlete, a musical prodigy, and be saving the world somehow."

"Well, you're the best one on the baseball team and you're doing great community service," I say. In freshman year alone, our class helped save the Bramble Library and then did a children's book drive. We gathered enough books to furnish a whole library for a school hit by the hurricane in Louisiana. My dear friend Sulamina Mum — she was our minister — and her husband, Riley, delivered the books themselves when they moved to the South last month. I miss Mum. I wish she'd write.

"Enough about school," JFK says, "this here is summer vacation. That's all I care about." He hands me an orange life jacket.

I take it like it's a tarantula.

"Willa." JFK shakes his head. "You're acting strange. You've sailed before, right?"

"Sure," I say, my fingers fumbling, snapping on the jacket like I'm strapping myself into the electric chair. *Just tell him the truth, Willa, he'll understand.*

"Well, don't you *like* to sail?" JFK says. "You don't seem psyched."

"Oh, no, I love it." *Liar.* I look away. My gaze lands on a sand creation someone made earlier. It's three-tiered like a wedding cake, decorated with shells. There are even two little plastic figures on top.

"Great, then," JFK says, smiling, snapping his jacket on, too. "You might want to leave those here," he says, pointing to my sandals.

I take them off and throw them on the sand. One lands on the cake-castle, knocking off one of the figures. *Oops, sorry.*

JFK pushes the boat into the water. "The wind is perfect right now." He adjusts some ropes. "Hand me the rudder, will you?"

I reach for something. It's the wrong thing.

"That's the daggerboard," JFK says, laughing. "You've done this before, right?"

"Yes, I told you. What do you think, I'm lying?" *Now I definitely can't back out.*

JFK is staring at me. "Are you sure you're okay with this?"

The wind lifts my hair. "Yes, fine, let's go." *Be brave, Willa, be brave.*

"You get in first and I'll push us out," JFK says.

The boat rocks gently when I get in. It rocks more when he heaves himself in and sits beside me. His arm feels safe and strong next to mine. *Fine, this is going to be fine.*

With one hand, JFK releases the rope. The sail puffs with wind and we're off. With the other hand he moves the rudder and steers us out onto the open sea.

"When's the last time you went sailing?" JFK says.

We're already passing a buoy. I'm in way over my head. My hands are gripping the hull. "It's been a few years." I don't look at him.

"Well, nothing's changed," JFK says, all happy and proud, captain of his ship. "Wind is wind. When I say duck, duck."

Duck, duck, silly goose, Willa Havisham. What were you worrying about? See how nice this is? Safe and slow, no worries.

"Beautiful," JFK says, smiling. "I love this."

He releases the line some more and the sail billows full and now we are *moving*, moving fast. "Nice," he shouts, laughing. "Isn't this great?"

"Yeah," I manage to say. Then I think about the jellyfish that summer when I was ten. I had just gotten my Red Cross swimming certificate, passed with flying colors, and Nana allowed me to swim out to the buoy line. I was so happy, free as a fish, when a stinging pain like a needle shot into my arm. It stunned me and I panicked. I started flailing around in the water, trying to see what had bitten me. Was it a shark? A whole school of them? What if they were surrounding me? I screamed for help, HELP, waving frantically toward Nana on the shore. She waved back. *She thinks I'm waving!* I was too far out for her to hear me over the sounds of the waves and all of the people on the beach. It was early June, before the lifeguards ascended their thrones. I waved and waved and Nana waved back. *No, I'm not waving, I'm dying! Help! Oh, my gosh,* I thought, *what if I die out here?* And then I thought of my birthfather, Billy Havisham, who actually did die at sea when his hot air balloon crashed into the Atlantic Ocean the day after he and Mom married. His body was never found. . . .

"*Willa! Willa!* What's wrong with you!" JFK is shouting at me.

"I . . . I . . . nothing." I manage a smile, gripping the hull so tightly my hands are numb.

Faster and faster. Wind zipping through my air. Sea spray on my face.

"Whoo-hoo!" JFK shouts, his face beaming bright.

We're speeding now. *It's okay. Be brave, Willa, be brave.*

Our side of the boat rises high in the air, then higher, higher, higher, as the sail strains full with wind.

JFK's laughing. "Yes! Ha-ha! This is it!"

Then the wind changes and the sail wobbles and *wooshhhhhhes.* "Duck!" JFK shouts.

I freeze.

"Duck! Willa, now, watch out!"

JFK pushes me down hard, just before the sail swings over my head.

"Jeez, Willa," JFK says, laughing. He reaches out a hand to help me back up. "That's a good way to get beheaded."

"*Take me back!*" I scream. "*Now!*"

"Willa, what's wrong?" He looks shocked. "It's okay. I know what I'm doing."

"Take me back. I mean it." My body is shaking, scared.

"Now, Joseph, please."

Back at the shore, I tell him about the jellyfish and how I haven't swum over my head in the ocean since, and how I still have nightmares about my birthfather, swimming terrified out in the raging sea, engulfed by house-size waves.

"But, I've seen you swimming," JFK says. "You're like a fish at Dean's Pond."

"That's a lake," I explain. "It's ocean swimming

I'm scared of. I'm okay if I can stand. It's when I get over my head that I panic."

"We weren't going to tip," JFK says. "I've been sailing since I was seven. I know what I'm doing. And besides, why didn't you just tell me?" There's an edge of anger in his voice.

I'm expecting him to be sympathetic. Here I just poured out my heart to him.

"Why did you lie to me, Willa," he says, standing up. "Don't you trust me?"

"I'm sorry."

"I said, don't you trust me?"

"Joseph, yes, of course I do."

"Well, you have a weird way of showing it. Come on, hop out."

I step out into the shallow water and walk up onto the beach with shaky legs.

JFK pulls the boat up onshore. He wraps a wire around the rudder and centerboard and locks them, stuffs the life jackets underneath the hull.

"Come on," he says. "I'll take you home."

"Joseph, please. Don't be mad."

"It's all right," he says.

"We still have time," I say. "Why don't we go for a walk or something?"

"No, I'm going home for dinner. Coach wants us over to the field early. We're working concessions for the Cape League game tonight."

"Why don't I meet you there," I say.

JFK still looks mad. "No. I mean, you can do what you want, but I won't be able to hang out. Like I said, I'll be doing concessions."

"Okay, sure," I say.

When we bike up to the inn, I say, "Call me?"

"Yeah, sure, Willa. See ya later."

After dinner, I pull out my journal. I always feel better when I write, especially if I'm down. I pour all my mucky feelings about today with JFK out on the page.

Learn a lesson from this, Willa. You've got to trust the people you love.

I stare at that word "love" for a long time. What does that even mean?

Someone's knocking on my door.

"Willa," Darryl says. Darryl is front desk manager tonight. "You have a friend downstairs."

"Thanks, Darryl." *Tina, yes.* I slip my journal into the hiding spot between the mattress and box spring. Tina will know exactly how to handle my fiasco with JFK.

Tina Belle understands the mysteries of the male mind.

CHAPTER 6

No Mutts About It

Two may talk and one may hear,
but three cannot take part in a conversation
of the most sincere and searching sort.
— Ralph Waldo Emerson

As soon as we're up in my room, Tina closes the door and says, "Guess what? Big news. Ruby's family just bought the house next door to you."

"Which one?" I ask.

"The one where you and Stella used to live before she married Sam," Tina answers.

"What? *Why?* The Sivlers live in a mansion."

I go to my window and look across the wide, green lawn, over at the stately brick house that was my first home in Bramble. It's been vacant since Mom and I moved in here with Sam.

"The Sivlers aren't going to *live* there," Tina says, laughing.

"So they're going to rent it out?"

"Nope," Tina says, plopping down on my bed, smiling like a toddler with a secret. "Keep guessing. This is fun. See if you can figure out what they're opening there."

"Opening? So, it's a business? I don't think they can do that. This is a residential area."

"Actually," Tina says in a serious tone, all proud that she has insider information, "I heard Ruby's parents talking about that very thing. Mr. Sivler said the building is 'zoned commercial.' Your mother ran Weddings by Havisham on the first floor. That was a business. And before you moved here, it was a funeral home."

"Oh, right," I say. "I remember the Realtor telling us about the funeral home thing when we took the lease. I was a little spooked at first, but then I forgot about it. Wait . . . they're not opening a *funeral home*, are they?"

Tina giggles. "Yeah, right," she says, enjoying this. "No. Come on, Willa, seven questions. You win, I buy you a sundae at Bloomin' Jean's. I win, you buy me a water. I'm on a diet. Deal?"

"Deal."

"Done."

"Okay," I say. "Is it a restaurant?"

"No." Tina shakes her head. "That's one."

"A clothing store?"

"No. That's two."

"I can count, Tina. Is it a jewelry store?"

"No. That's three."

"Is there another business like it already in Bramble?"

"Good question, Willa. No. That's four."

Hmmm. "Is it a product place or a service place?"

"Excellent question," Tina says. "Well, I'm sure they'll have products for sale, but the main thing is service. And, by the way, that's five."

"A service, *hmmmm*, I'm thinking a spa, but there's already the Sea Spa in town and you said there wasn't anything like it in Bramble. Is it a service I would use?"

Tina giggles. "No, definitely not. That's six. Give up?"

"No. I get one more question." I think about the Sivlers. How loud and flashy they are. Mrs. Sivler wearing low-cut tops, slinky skirts, and spiked heels at Bramble Academy events and on Sunday at BUC, rhymes with luck, our nondenominational community church.

There's a knock on the door. "Yes?" I say.

Sam pops his head in. "Oh, hi, Tina."

"Hi, Mr. Gracemore. I like the new flower boxes out front."

"Thank you, Tina," he says, smiling. "Willa, there's someone downstairs for you."

"Thanks, Dad."

He closes the door.

"*Dad?*" Tina says. "Since when are you calling Sam, Dad?"

"Since Father's Day."

"Oh, that's so sweet," Tina says, fixing her hair in the mirror. "It's probably Joseph downstairs."

"No, Sam would have said. And besides, Joseph's mad at me." I quickly tell her the sailing story.

"I don't blame you, Willa," Tina says, ever the best friend taking my side. "You wouldn't catch me out on one of those little Sunfishes, either. They look like baby bathtub boats for gosh sakes. If a real boat gets too close, you're in with the fish. Yachts are much more civilized. You've been out on our *Salty Princess*. Now that's a boat. You can sprawl out and sunbathe on the deck, have a formal dinner down below, shower, sleep —"

"Come on, Tina," I say. "Let's see who's downstairs." Tina follows me.

It's Mariel Sanchez. She's in the game room, playing cards with the Red Hat ladies. The women are decked out in purple outfits with red cowboy hats, all set to head out to the Garth Brooks concert at the Melody Tent.

Mariel waves and smiles when she sees us.

"Hi, Mare," I say.

"Willa . . . Tina . . . hi." Mare stands up from the card table. "Gotta go, ladies, good-bye. Have fun tonight, and don't do anything I wouldn't do." The Red Hats laugh.

Mare walks toward me and Tina, smiling. "I was dropping off books at the library. Thought you might want to catch the baseball game or get an ice cream."

"Actually, that's where we were headed," I say.

Mare looks at Tina. "I saw you and Ruby at the beach today."

"Yeah, I saw you, too," Tina says. She looks down at Mariel's feet.

Mariel is wearing sneakers, not Swiss cheese sandals like us.

"Are you a member of the BBA?" Tina asks Mariel.

That's short for Bramble Beach Association. Tina knows Mariel isn't.

"No," Mare says. "Why?"

"Because Sandy Beach is privately owned and —"

"Hey, girls," I say, interrupting. "Baseball or ice cream?" I move into the center between them as we walk into town. I'm hoping they say baseball so I can see JFK.

"Let's hit Bloomin' Jean's first, then head over to the field," Tina says, flipping her hair back, decision done. "Ruby's father is sponsoring the game tonight."

We walk toward the ice cream parlor in silence.

"So, Tina," I say, "you didn't tell me. How do the lifeguards look this year?"

"Same as always," Tina answers.

Several more seconds of silence. "Mariel," I say, "Tina was telling me about a new business moving in next door to our inn."

"Really," Mare says, leaning around me to look at Tina. "That's interesting, what?"

Tina shrugs her shoulders.

"Come on, Tina," I say. "Give it up. Dish the news."

Tina gives me an annoyed look. "It's nothing important."

"Well then, what is it?" Mariel says.

Tina just keeps walking.

"Come on, Tina," I say jokingly, "don't make me beg like a dog."

"It's a pet spa," Tina blurts out. "They're opening a pet spa. No big deal."

I stop walking. Mare does, too. Tina stops, then turns back to look at us.

"What do you mean . . . a *pet spa*?" Mariel asks.

Tina leans in dramatically toward Mariel, eyes squinching like Mare is from Mars. "You *do know* what a spa is, right?"

Uh-oh. I intervene. "So they're opening a place to bring dogs to get groomed."

Tina huffs disgustedly. "You can do *that* at the mall, Willa. No Mutts About It will be a four-star luxury resort for our four-legged friends. Beauty treatments, massages, overnight lodging in private suites, gourmet room service dining . . ."

"For *dogs*?" Mariel says, appalled.

I picture the cramped room where Mariel's entire family is living in that ugly old run-down motel on the edge of town, all they can afford even though their father works full-time . . . warming up meals in a microwave, no kitchen . . .

"Yes," Tina says, hands on her hips. "Do you have a problem with that?"

"Yes," Mariel says in a quiet voice. "I do."

"You know what, Willa," Tina says. "I'm not into

ice cream anymore. I'll catch up with you guys at the game."

"Tina, wait." She doesn't stop.

"I'm sorry, Willa," Mariel says quietly. "Go with your friend."

"No," I say. "That's all right. I have a problem with the pet spa, too."

When Mariel and I get to the field, they are just finishing the national anthem, and the announcer is saying that this evening's game is courtesy of The Sivler Group, the holding company for Sivler Realty and Construction and several other Bramble businesses including the soon to be opened No Mutts About It. "And, everyone, please join me now in a big Bramble welcome for Miss Ruby Sivler, who will be throwing out the first ball tonight."

Mariel and I watch as Ruby swaggers out onto the green, bopping in a tight red tank top, hips swaying in a short skirt. She smiles, flashing her newly whitened teeth. There's an explosion of whistles and catcalls. Ruby waves up to the bleachers, blowing kisses. I look at Mariel and we roll our eyes.

Ruby holds up the ball, arches her arm back, up, and

over, and lets it go. The catcher catches the ball and the crowd applauds. The announcer shouts, "Play ball!"

"Where do you want to sit?" Mariel says.

I see Tina right above the dugouts, sitting with Mrs. Sivler and Ruby's older sister, who's home for the summer from college. No Mutts About It, my butt. I have no interest in talking to that family. "Wherever," I say. "It doesn't matter."

"I love baseball," Mariel says, as we find seats several rows up.

"Well, you've moved to the right place, then," I say. "The Cape Cod Baseball League is famous. Some of the best players in the country start out here."

At the end of the third inning, Mariel goes to the restroom and I go to the concession stand to look for JFK. There's a long line. When I get to him, he acts nice enough, but I can tell he's still mad. He hands me the soda and takes my money.

"Joseph, hi!" Mare comes up behind me.

"Hey, Mare," JFK says, smiling, all happy to see her.

"I didn't know you worked here," Mare says.

"I don't," JFK says. "Our team is just helping out tonight."

"I wanted to tell you," Mariel says. "I got that job at Stop 'N Shop you were telling me about. I won't be fifteen until the end of August, but after your mother called the manager, they said I could start next week. Tell your mom I said thanks, okay?"

"Sure, Mare," JFK says. "But you should stop by and tell her yourself. She always likes to see you."

Jealousy pops up, but I push it back down. *JFK and Mare are just friends, that's all. Remember, Willa? You've been through this already. Just friends.*

"Oh, and, Joe," Mariel says, "did you decide about the audition for . . ."

What audition?

"Hey, hey, hey," a guy behind us shouts. "Hurry up. I need a hot dog. If you want to sit around chatting, go to a soccer game. This is *baseball*."

After the game, I try to find JFK, but by the time I make my way down the bleachers and through the crowd, when I get to the concession stand, he's gone.

Later, I call his cell phone, but he doesn't answer. I check, but he's not online.

CHAPTER 7

Beauty and the Bites

Nature and books belong to the eyes that see them.
— Ralph Waldo Emerson

The next morning I wake up in a slump. First I mess things up with JFK, then I push Tina even further away, and what if Mariel and JFK really start liking each other? I know Mare's my friend, but she's gorgeous. I don't want her over at my boyfriend's house, even if it is just to visit his mother.

It's only four A.M. Sunday. Bramble United Community, BUC, rhymes with luck, is at eleven. I wonder who the new minister is? Whoever it is won't ever replace Sulamina Mum. Mum was my first friend in Bramble, almost like another mother to me. I miss her, but I couldn't be happier that she and Riley finally got together. They were high school sweethearts, separated by the war, and time, and geography, but I worked a bit of Cape-cupid matchmaking magic, and the two of them got together. All I did was nudge Mum until she wrote him a letter. Her words did all the rest. Never underestimate the power of a letter.

I flick on the light by my bed and open up today's book, *True Believer*, by Virginia Euwer Wolff. I had scanned the cover in Nana's store and it looked good. I open to the first page:

"*My name is LaVaughn and I am 15. When a little kid draws a picture it is all a big face and some arms stuck on. That's their life. Well, then: You get older and you are a whole mess of things, new thoughts, sorry feelings, big plans, enormous doubts, going along hoping and getting disappointed, over and over again...*"

Nice, I'm hooked already. I like when an author writes in "first person." It lets me feel like I'm right inside that character, feeling all the things she's feeling.

I read for a half hour or so, and then remember I need a new quote for the Bramble Board. I reach for Emerson. Old Ralph's quite the quotable guy. Here's a good one:

"The only true gift is a portion of yourself."

That sounds like something Sulamina Mum would say. She always had a subtle, or sometimes not-so-subtle, way of reminding us to "get out of our selves" and focus on others, finding ways to serve. Sam calls that "community rent." Just like you pay rent for housing, you should pay rent to your community, too, by giving a portion of your time or money or talents to help others.

This past spring I wrote an editorial letter to the *Cape Times* about the shortage of affordable housing on the Cape — seeing Mariel's living conditions made me look into the issue — and my small letter sparked something big. It inspired a recently retired couple, the Barretts from New Seabury, to set up a fund to help build homes for low-income families. My "talent" was writing the letter. Sam says words can have a powerful effect. Think about the book *Charlotte's Web*, and those two little words: "some pig."

If Mum was here, she'd say, "Nice job with that letter, Willa, but what are you going to do next? *Hmmm*, you have a big, long summer ahead. What, two whole months at least, right? The work is never done, little sister. Don't go hiding your light like an ostrich in the sand. Go find your next way to shine."

I look at the clock. Five A.M. Maybe I'm not too late for the sunrise. I jump out of bed, pull on shorts and a shirt. Grab my journal and a water bottle in the kitchen, toss them in the wicker basket on my bike outside, and take off quick for the beach.

It's dark and quiet, like I'm the only person awake in the world. Then a bird sings down to me from the telephone wire above and I realize I'm not alone. As I near the water, a soft mist coats my face. The sky is filmy and cotton candy pink.

When I reach the beach, I look out at the horizon. *Yes.* I'm not too late. And, *good*, no one else is here. I sit on the top step and stare out at the scene before me. Beauty, beauty, everywhere . . . The sea is calm, silver colored, flat like a mirror, peaceful. How silly to be so scared sailing with JFK. And Mariel, look at how she snorkeled without fear. I wonder what it would be like to see that whole other world beneath the waves. I bet it's beautiful.

A fish tail breaks the surface, then bobs back underneath. *Ouch.* Something bit my neck. I slap it. A tiny black bug. *Ouch*, another bit my head. I scratch. Then there's a bunch of them all around my face. Oh, great. I flap my hands. It doesn't make a difference. *Ouch.* I wish I had bug spray.

Down below, a little black-capped tern, one of the endangered birds, hovers in the air above the water, searching for food. It flaps crazily in the air, fighting the wind, trying to stay in place, hovering like a helicopter waiting to land. It spots its prey and nose-dives into the water, then comes right back up again, empty beaked. *Sorry, little tern.*

Now the sky is a palette of pinks and purples, getting brighter and brighter. It's almost time. *Ouch*, I slap my leg. If I can just withstand these stupid bugs. I scratch and scratch. And then, there it is. A sliver of sun, like a salmon.

Good morning, new day. Thank you.

As it rises, the sun casts a red line across the water to me, closer and closer until it reaches the shore, bearing a sheath of sparkling rubies. I close my eyes and scoop up the jewels, locking them safe in my memory.

I open my eyes and open my journal, writing fast to capture this moment.

It was worth the bug bites. That's the way life is. There is good and bad in everything. You can either focus on the annoying things you have no way of controlling, or cast your gaze upon the glory of a bright new amazing day, hours of delightful possibility, stretching out like a summer before you.

I read over what I wrote. It doesn't do the sunrise justice at all. Such powerful beauty in nature, and then I try to capture it and it sounds so small.

I flip off my sandals and walk. The cool sand feels good beneath my feet. I take deep breaths, in and out, in and out. I think about JFK and Tina and the pet spa. Knowing how she feels about animals, I'm not sure how to break the news to my mother. I let all these worries wash over me and then out to sea with the waves. I can't imagine a better way to start a day. Watching the sunrise and walking the beach. I'm a "lucky duck," as Nana would say.

Out on the end of the Spit, the area where the bird people were stringing the posts yesterday, there is a new sign. A large, pay-attention sign.

AREA CLOSED
Threatened Birds Nesting

Common Tern   Least Tern   Piping Plover

If birds are disturbed, parents may leave the nest,
subjecting eggs and young to exposure
and possible death.
Entering this area is a violation
of state and federal law.

These rare birds, their nests, and eggs are protected
under Massachusetts and federal laws.
Persons may be arrested and
fined for killing or harassing
or in any way disturbing birds nesting in this area.
Massachusetts Audubon Society

Just there, a few feet ahead of me, a piping plover is giving two babies a flying lesson out over the waves. I stand for a moment, watching. How beautiful they are. I wonder what Sam found out about that nasty flyer someone put on the Bramble Board.

I turn and head back along the water. I slip on my sandals, walk up the stairs. I think about Tina questioning Mariel about being on this beach, like she didn't have a right to be here. When I get to the top, I look out at the scene one last time.

The sky is white now, the sun a blazing yellow yolk. Like a perfectly poached Sunday brunch egg at the Bramblebriar Inn.

When I get home, I take out the silver box on the porch and grab the letters I need to change the Bramble Board. T, H, E, O, N, L, Y, T, R, U, E, G, I, F, T . . .

I stick on the letters and step back to read,

> "The only true gift is a portion of yourself."
> Ralph Waldo Emerson

The Shasta daisies Sam planted around the base of the Bramble Board are smiling up at me. I pick one and lift the sunny yellow center to my nose. I pluck the petals: *he loves me*, *he loves me not*, *he loves me*, *he loves me not.* . . . Suddenly, I have this strange feeling that someone is watching me.

I look over at my old house, soon to be the Sivlers' pet spa. Was that a curtain moving upstairs? I keep an eye on the second-floor window, which was my mother's bedroom. It's probably one of the renovation workers, painting or something. But who would be working this early in the morning? On a Sunday? That's weird.

I stand there staring for a few seconds. No more movement at the window. I'm sure I must have imagined it. I shake it off, toss the flower, and run up the stairs to make a cup of tea before church.

CHAPTER 8

"Family Day"

*I like the silent church before the service begins,
better than any preaching.*
— Ralph Waldo Emerson

As we're walking to BUC, I tell Sam about the endangered birds sign I saw posted out on the Spit.

Bramble United Community is a place where all people are welcome, no matter your background, no matter your beliefs. We come together once a week "to be grateful." Our former minister, Sulamina Mum, used to say the only prayer you ever need is just two words long: *Thank you.*

Jew, Catholic, Baptist, Buddhist, Atheist, Agnostic, or whatever "ist" you ist or isn't, we all share a common belief in the goodness of the human spirit, a gratitude for our lives, and a sense of responsibility to the greater world community.

"I asked around town yesterday, Willa," Sam says, "but I couldn't find out anything about that plover flyer. Probably just somebody's strange idea of a practical joke. I don't think it's anything more than that."

"But why did they post it on our Bramble Board?" I say.

"Because the board is Bramble's center of 'buzz,'" Sam says.

"Buzz" is way too corny for a father to be saying, but I don't roll my eyes.

"It's like what the inn guidebooks say about us," Sam says. "People read the Bramble Board to get inspired and to find out what's cooking around town."

"Cooking" is even cornier than "buzz," but I let Sam slide.

BUC isn't very crowded. Lots of locals vacation off-Cape in the summer to escape the clogged roads and crowded restaurants. Some people, especially those near the shore, rent their houses out to tourists in the summer.

Up at the pulpit, in a fancy black robe with a red velvet collar, is Dr. Theodore J. Deadham of Harvard Divinity School, "most recently of the First Unitarian Universalist Society of Boston." When he looks our way, I smile at him. He doesn't smile back.

Dr. Deadham reads his entire sermon in a loud, booming voice, without ever pausing to look at us. It's the worst service ever. That man found five ways to remind us he was from Harvard in the first five minutes, but didn't say anything I will remember. He might have the smartest brain on the planet, but he didn't move my heart at all.

I try to be open-minded, and openhearted, really I do — Mum would have demanded nothing less — but Dr. Deadham was so puffed up with his own self-importance, I fully expected him to sprout peacock feathers at any given moment. Blue, green, yellow, red.

"We should at least give him the benefit of a second chance," Sam says quietly as we congregate in the gathering space for bagels and donuts.

Sam is a teacher, so you have to forgive him. I think teachers are genetically wired to be kind and encouraging.

"Completely uninspiring" is my mother's more callous critique.

"Brainiac-boring" is Tina's two cents.

"Certainly an intelligent, well-read man" is my good friend, our librarian, Mrs. Saperstone's assessment, "but he unfortunately doesn't seem to have a sense of humor."

"I will reserve judgment until I've heard him speak

again," says Dr. Swaminathan, my English teacher at Bramble Academy. See what I mean about the genetic wiring? Dr. Swammy, who's such an amazing teacher, is just back from India. Sam filled in for him while he was away. It was cool having Sam as my teacher. I was so proud. I kept looking around the classroom, wanting to say, "Do you all realize this man is my father?"

"What did you think of Dr. Deadham, Willa?" Sam says as we're walking home.

"On a scale of one to ten, compared to Mum, I guess I'd give him a two."

"Two's too generous," Nana says. "But, that's the last we'll be seeing of the Doc, anyway."

"What do you mean, Nana?"

"I did a quick check-in with the other members of the BUC Board of Directors and there was an overwhelming consensus. We test out ministers and vote before we formally offer a candidate the position. This is a plum job, Willa. We're a great community here in Bramble. You know that. We won't settle for anything less than the best. We broke it to Dr. Dead gently. I bet he's halfway home to Beantown as we speak." Beantown is our nickname for Boston.

"I love you, Nana." I hug her, laughing.

We stop in front of Sweet Bramble Books. Nana lives upstairs from the store.

"Can you come by later, Willa?" Nana says. "I'm gearing up for the vote and I need your help."

Nana's not talking politics. She's talking taffy. Saltwater taffy, that is. I'm her official "taste tester" for trying out new flavors each season. *Cape Cod Life* magazine does a readers' "best of" survey. Nana's neck and neck with Ghelfi's of Mashpee for "Best Sweets on the Upper Cape." She wants to win best bookstore, too, but there are so many other good bookstores, that would be tough. No way is she going to beat them. So with the "best of" survey, we've got all our eggs in the candy basket, so to speak.

"Ghelfi's has a gorgeous new window display, just for taffy," Nana says, all worried, "and they've got slick new ads boasting their fifty-two varieties of taffy, the largest selection of any candy store on the Cape. How can I compete with that?"

"Let me think about it, Nana," I say. "I can't come today, but I'll come first thing tomorrow, promise."

Just recently, my mother has officially claimed Sunday as "Family Day." When we get back to the inn, Mom checks to make sure everyone has shown up for work and that there are no pressing issues she has to attend to.

"Go, Stella," Darryl says, sweetly shooing my mother away from the front desk. "It's your day with your family. Go, enjoy."

I'm fairly sure my mother read something in one of her trusted business magazines about the importance of scheduling a "family activity" every weekend. Last Sunday we took the ferry out to Nantucket, the island where Mom and Sam eloped to. Such a pretty place, so romantic. I'm glad I got to see it.

I don't mind "Family Day," but today all I want to do is see JFK and make sure he's not mad at me anymore. And Tina, I need to talk to Tina. And Mariel. What audition was she talking to JFK about?

"So what's the plan, ma'am?" Sam says to my mother with a smile.

"A bike ride on the Rail Trail?" Mom suggests, consulting a paper that is probably her summer "to do" list of family activities.

"Sounds good," Sam says, patting his stomach. "I could use some exercise. Couldn't resist a second helping of the filet mignon last night. Okay with you, Willa?"

"Sure," I say, "but just not all day. There are some things I need to do later."

Sam and Mom look at each other and smile.

"Teenagers," my mother whispers, shaking her head.

I roll my eyes to myself. Lately, I'm starting to feel like a bit of an outsider. Mom and Sam are united, a team — "Let me talk with your father first," or "Let me just run this by your mother." We're all on the same field. But they're on one team, and I'm on the other.

The Cape Cod Rail Trail is a network of paved bike trails that run through some of the nicest nature you've ever seen. After the railroads stopped running on the Cape years ago, someone had the excellent idea to pull up the tracks and pave over them. The Rail Trail starts in Dennis and weaves through forests and fields, along marshes and cranberry bogs, past harbors and ponds (that's what we call lakes), through towns and villages, past country stores and ice cream places, all the way out to Wellfleet.

Sam puts our bikes on the rack of his car and we drive to a Rail Trail parking lot.

As we get on our bikes, I see Sam wink at my mother and my mother smile back at him. They are so in love. I can't help but think about the baby they lost. It would have been nice to have a little brother or sister. I've been an only child my whole life. Maybe Aunt Ruthie and Spruce will have kids. Then I'll have cousins or saplings or something.

"I'll race you," Stella shouts, and we're off.

I love this family.

CHAPTER 9

Beach Rights

Mine, and yours;
Mine, not yours.
Earth endures;
Stars abide —
Shine down in the old sea.

— Ralph Waldo Emerson

When we get home, hot and sweaty from biking, Mom suggests we go to the beach. I'm about to decline, when I see the look on her face. She seems so happy and relaxed. This family time stuff is important to her, and anyway, I'm sure Tina will be at the beach, stalking lifeguards, and I need to talk with her.

Mom and I head upstairs to change. Sam says he'll pack sandwiches.

When we get to the beach, we pause at the top of the stairs. Out on the Spit, there's a red light swirling on the harbormaster's boat and a large group of people all huddled together.

"Let's see what's going on," Mom says.

At the bottom of the stairs, I spot Tina and Ruby. They are standing at the base of a lifeguard chair, staring up at a greased Greek god of a guy. Ruby says something and the god leans down to answer. Tina smiles, nodding her head, then writes something on a clipboard like she's taking notes. I wonder what that's all about.

Mom and Sam and I walk out on the Spit.

As we approach the crowd, we hear shouting. I notice someone has ripped down the ropes and stakes from the piping plover and tern nesting area.

"Look at that," Sam says.

There is black paint smeared over the new Audubon Society warning sign.

"Who's gonna make me?" a big-bellied man with a very red face is shouting.

"It's just for a few weeks, maybe a month," says a young, college-age-looking woman wearing a brown uniform shirt with the official Audubon seal on the pocket.

"This is *our* beach," a lady shouts. It's Ruby Sivler's mother, perched on the hull of their yacht, all tanned in a shiny pink bikini. "We already have people sneaking onto this beach who don't belong here, taking up space. Sometimes we can't even find a place to sit."

"That's right!" someone shouts.

"But what about the birds?" a boy says.

"I don't give a flying —"

"But these aren't just any old birds," the Audubon lady says. "The least and common terns and the piping plovers are on the endangered species list."

An adult plover is hovering in the air by the shoreline, screeching. It circles around and soars in toward us, swiping close to Mrs. Sivler's bright red hair.

"Get away, get away," Mrs. Sivler screams, flapping her arms hysterically. "These birds are dangerous! They don't belong here!"

"They won't attack you," the Audubon worker explains. "It's just a mother trying to scare you away from her chicks, that's all."

"We have a right to enjoy our beach," Mrs. Sivler says, picking up her fluffy white poodle, Pookie, and hugging him to her chest. People . . . and their pets . . . come before *birds*."

"That's right," a man with a sunburned face shouts, "people count more than plovers."

I wonder if he's the one who put the flyer on our Bramble Board? Or, wait, what if it was Mrs. Sivler?

"We all have a right to this beach," a college kid says, putting his arm around his girlfriend.

"Excuse me," Ruby Sivler's father says, standing up on his boat, cocking his captain's hat to the side, and speaking with great authority, "but that's not true. Only those property owners between Sea Bluff and Windy Road, and Shore Drive and Oak Path have actual, legally deeded rights to this beach."

"That's right!" a lady shouts. "I had to tell some boy to leave the other day. He was building a fire, all set to cook a fish, and his dog was running loose. I told him this was private property."

"Good for you," Mr. Sivler says. "We need to protect our investment from trespassers. It's high time we institute an identification system so we know who belongs here and who doesn't."

"Hear, hear," some man shouts. A few people clap.

I spot Mariel in the crowd. She steps forward, hands on her hips. "With all due respect, sir, if anybody owns this beach, it's the Wampanoag Indians you stole it from. They were here before the Pilgrims landed. Centuries before any of you."

Yay, Mariel. You tell him. I start to walk toward her and then stop and turn at the sound of barking.

There's a huge, golden-brown shaggy dog sniffing around dangerously close to one of the silver cages the Audubon workers put over the eggs and newly hatched chicks.

"Get that dog on a leash!" someone shouts.

The dog nudges the cage as if he's trying to flip it over.

The guy with the red face claps. "That's right! Show those birds who's top dog around here."

"Is that your dog, sir?" Sam asks the man in a calm voice.

"Not mine," the guy says.

The dog runs over to where Sam and Mom and I are standing. It shakes its coat and water sprays on my legs. Then the dog hunches down and poops right in front of us.

"That's disgusting," Mom says, looking around at the faces. "Who owns this dog? Dogs aren't allowed on this beach without a leash. It's against the law."

The dog looks at me. Our eyes lock for a second. It doesn't have a collar. Then, I know this sounds silly, but I swear the dog smiles at me, a big goofy clownish smile like that carnival booth at the Barnstable Fair where you throw three balls into the clown's mouth to win a stuffed animal prize.

The dog turns and runs up over the dune and is gone.

We stop at Bobby Byrne's restaurant in Mashpee Commons for dinner. I like how they have quotes from famous writers on the walls here. I order a cup of clam chowder — we call it "chowda" — and the Shakespeare chicken sandwich. *Yumm.*

Next, I do some undercover sleuthing at Ghelfi's candy store. They've added on and remodeled. They're even serving ice cream now. I get the vanilla frozen yogurt with Heath bar chunks, my favorite.

I take a long time making my saltwater taffy selections, making mental notes on all their new flavors. No way can Nana compete with their variety. We'll need to think of a different angle.

Back home, I run up to my room and close the door. I take out my cell phone and call JFK. All I get is his voice, with rap music in the background. "Hey, this is Joe; I'm not around, so leave me a message." *Beep.*

"Hi, Joseph. It's Willa. Listen, I'm sorry again about yesterday. Call me, okay?"

I check, but he's not online, either. I leave a message there, too.

Aunt Ruthie's wedding. Even though my heart's not in it, I get out her letter and my planning notebook.

She said she wants something simple and outdoors. I think Sam's backyard Labyrinth will be perfect. The daisies and dahlias and brown-eyed Susans are in full bloom, and if we do it at six, we'll still have plenty of light. Ruthie's note says her friend Michael is a minister and will officiate the ceremony. Note: Ask Sam what kind of music Ruthie likes.

Now for the menu. I head down to the kitchen and browse through the cookbooks. I pull three vegetarian titles from the shelf and start looking for recipes. Let's see, first course. Gazpacho would be a good choice . . . or, maybe a chilled blueberry soup? Salad . . . fresh garden greens and chèvre cheese. And, Sam's famous Bramblebriar bruschetta, with fresh tomatoes and basil. The main course is harder. Everything I think of has meat or fish. Tofu turkey? No. Maybe a pasta of some sort? Here's a good one: angel-hair pasta with fresh grilled red and yellow peppers, asparagus, and mozzarella. *Mmmm, yum.*

The dessert is a piece of cake, literally. Rosie will be whipping up the signature Bramblebriar Inn wedding cake with the lucky charms in the center well. When Rosie bakes her famous cake, she leaves a hollow space — a "wishing well," I call it — in the top tier of the cake, so that I can add twelve little silver charms. A book, a rose, an angel, a butterfly, an anchor, a rainbow . . . The cake was Rosie's idea, the charms were mine. It's our new old-fashioned wedding custom. Each tiny charm is wrapped in a piece of plastic with a satin ribbon attached. I put the charms in the well, and we drape the ribbons up and out over the tiers of the cake like a waterfall. At the reception, twelve pennies are randomly placed under dinner plates around the room. Those twelve people get to pull a good luck charm from the cake. So far, guests seem to love this new tradition at Bramblebriar. I like listening to people assign meanings to the charms they pull.

"Oh, it's a butterfly! I bet that means . . ."

Back upstairs, I turn on my night-light, open up my bag of candy and *True Believer*. I am loving this book.

Hours later, I'm finished. I'm sad because I want to read on and on. There's this one scene in which the main character, LaVaughn, has gone through a really hard time. She's been holding something inside that

she's been afraid to tell her mother, but finally she does
and her mother rises to the occasion:

> "Maybe it was hours she held me there,
>   maybe only minutes.
> And then she fed me supper in bed,
> her good beef and mushrooms;
> she pulled up a chair to my desk and we ate
>   there in my room
> with the weeping willow tree hanging over."

I close the book and put it on my Willa's Pix shelf.
The battle on the beach over the birds comes into
my mind. I open up my journal to write.

*Who owns a beach? Who owns the ocean? Who
owns any part of the earth? Do people have any
more right to any of it than plants or animals do?
Just because we're bigger, does that make us better? Dinosaurs were bigger and look what happened
to them.*

I think about the funny, shaggy dog who smiled
at me. . . .
I yawn, close my journal, and shut off the light.
I'll figure it all out tomorrow.

CHAPTER 10

Everyone's Writing Books

Meek young men grow up in libraries,
Believing it their duty to accept the views which
Cicero, which Locke, which Bacon have given,
Forgetful that Cicero, Locke and Bacon were
only young men in libraries when they wrote these
books.

— Ralph Waldo Emerson

Monday morning I'm on breakfast duty with Mom and Makita. Rosie tells me what the specials are, and I write the choices on the chalkboards in the dining room and out on the sunporch:

* Cranberry-nut pancakes with Vermont maple syrup
* Cheddar cheese, apple, and sausage omelet
with cinnamon-swirl toast
* Blueberry yogurt with honey-nut granola and berries
* * * Muffin du jour: Cherry-chocolate * * *

"*Cherry-chocolate muffins?* I better taste test these first," I say, pouring myself a cup of tea from the white china pot with the blue-and-green flowers, a gift from Nana last Christmas. Nana insists the only civilized way to drink tea is from a teapot, none of that dunking a bag in a mug of microwaved hot water stuff.

The tea has been steeping for three minutes and is now a perfect reddish brown. I add a little milk — no sugar, just milk — that's the way Nana and I take our tea. Gramp Tweed and I used to drink lemon tea together, no milk, when we did our Friday after-noon "book-talks" on the couch at Sweet Bramble Books. It's funny how we have different customs with the different people in our lives. Sam drinks "Yogi" tea, gingerroot is his favorite. I like it, too. The bags have little messages on them like fortune cookie bits of wisdom. Sam puts the messages he likes best on the counter in the kitchen. *Hey, that gives me an idea for Nana. . . .*

I bite into the cherry-chocolate muffin, still warm from the oven, and quickly plop down on a chair before I faint from happiness. "Oh, my gosh, Rosie! These are *amazing.*" I lick the chocolate from my fingers. The taste reminds me of the chocolate-covered cherry cor-dials I used to love. Until they got me into trouble with my mother and ruined the most important wedding of her career — well, that's a whole other story. Now, saltwater taffy is my favorite candy. Cape Cod is famous for it.

"Really, Rosie," I say. "These muffins are to die for."

"Thank you, Willa," Rosie says. She steals a glance at my mother, who is filling wicker baskets with muffins, covering each basket with a green linen napkin.

"Rosie," I say. "You should write a cookbook. I meant what I said. I'm going to see my grandmother later. I could ask her if —"

"Willa," my mother says loudly, cutting me off. "Please start around with the coffee."

Out on the sunporch, I look out the window. There are several trucks parked in front of our old brick house, soon to be No Mutts About It. The front door is open and the shades are all up. There are workers inside painting. Two guys are on the roof fixing something. My eyes land on my mother's old bedroom window where I thought I saw someone yesterday.

It's the only window with the curtains drawn. Strange.

"More coffee?" I say, circulating the porch with pots of regular and decaf, cheerfully wishing our guests good morning and inquiring how their vacations are going.

The Red Hat ladies are gushing about the concert. "Garth's a god," Mrs. Madden says, fanning her face with an autographed picture. "Worth every penny." The ladies are taking the ferry out to Martha's Vineyard this morning and then going to a program at the Bramble Library tonight. Our town librarian, my friend Mrs. Saperstone, is doing her annual "Bramble Beach Reads" suggested list of good summer books. The Moscatellos are heading up to Provincetown for a whale watch. "Don't forget to climb Pilgrim Monument," I say. "The view from up top is beautiful. And be sure to stop at the National Seashore on the way home. It's something you absolutely don't want to miss."

Sam is in the corner talking with new guests who checked in last night. He introduces me to Fred and Pauline Miller and their children, Kamen and Shay.

"Mr. Miller was just telling me about his new book," Sam says.

"Cool," I say. "What's it about?"

"About reaching our fullest potential," Mr. Miller says, "and helping other people reach theirs."

"Sounds interesting," I say. "What's it called?"

Mr. Miller laughs. "My editor's still deciding, but the working title is *Be Big*."

"*Be Big*," I say. "Nice. I'd like to read it."

"Me, too," Sam says. "Let us know when it's out, Fred. We'll definitely need a signed copy for the inn library and one for the Bramble Library, too."

Sam and I carry trays out to the kitchen. He looks lost in thought.

"What about you, Dad? Aren't you working on a book?"

He doesn't respond.

I continue, "That first night you invited me and Mom here for dinner, when you two were first dating, you showed us your study. I remember your desk was covered with papers and there were manuscripts piled high on the floor. You said you were working on a book. But now you never talk about it anymore."

Sam looks at me and then away. "It's tough to break in to the book world, Willa. I'm not sure I have the talent. Maybe someday I'll get back to it."

"Of course you have the talent," I say. "You should be writing. Why aren't you?"

"There's never enough time, Willa. Running the inn is a full-time job. I had no idea we'd become so popular so fast."

Sam doesn't look happy about our success.

"Wait," I say, surprised. "Aren't you *happy* doing this? Opening the inn was Mom's idea, but I thought you enjoyed it, too. I know you miss teaching and if you want to be writing, you should have time for that, right? I would love to read some of your —"

"That's enough, Willa."

Sam's voice is sharp. Wow. He never talks like that to me.

"I'm sorry, Willa," he says. "It's just . . . I don't want to talk about it." Then, he smiles that beautiful Sam smile, his blue eyes framed with crinkles of kindness.

I smile back at him and let it go.

Later, biking to Tina's house, all I can think of is, *What is Sam's book about?*

When I get to Tina's, her mother tells me that Tina is at Ruby's house. I try not to show how sad that makes me feel.

"Go ahead over, Willa," Mrs. Belle says. "I know Tina would be sorry if she missed you."

Ruby and Tina are coming out of the Sivlers' front door when I arrive. Ruby has a camera and a notebook. Tina is carrying that clipboard I saw her with on the beach. They're laughing, all happy together. *BFF.*

I turn green. Not on the outside, of course, but sick-green to my stomach inside. Whoever named jealousy that color was right on the money. I'm guessing Shakespeare, but I'll have to look it up. Jealousy isn't pink or purple, definitely not yellow. It's green for sure. I think of Sam calling Ruthie a lean-green-mean-machine. Can't wait to meet her. I sure hope she likes the plans I've made for her wedding.

"Willa!" Tina shouts. "Guess what? We're making a book!"

"What kind of book?" It seems everyone's writing a book but me.

"A beach book," Ruby says in a superior voice. She adjusts something on her camera and then checks her nails.

"Well, more like a yearbook," Tina explains, "with photos and profiles of all the cutest lifeguards on Cape Cod, and room for autographs."

So that's what they were doing yesterday.

"We started with the boys on Sandy Beach," Ruby says. "That boy Desmond, from Dartmouth, is *delicious*, isn't he, Teen?"

"So hot he's on fire," Tina says. "That boy ought to

come with a warning label." They laugh like they've got a secret.

"Today we're headed up to Chatham," Ruby says.

"We're checking out one beach a day," Tina says.

I'm reading a book a day. Tina's reviewing a beach a day. I feel the space between us widening.

"It'll be hard doing so much research," Tina says. "I mean, who wants to work in the summer?"

Ruby laughs. "Yes, it will be horribly hard work chatting up beautiful boys in bathing suits every day, but hey, that's the price one pays for fame."

They crack up. I back away.

Tina looks at me. "Come with us, Willa." She doesn't sound like she means it.

"No, thanks," I answer. "I have to help my grandmother with something."

"Testing out new taffies?" Tina says.

Ruby giggles.

"Yeah, something like that."

"Wait, that reminds me," Ruby says. "Come on inside for a minute, Willa."

The Sivlers' kitchen is as spacious as a hotel lobby. On top of the long granite island in the center of the room there are water bottles of various sizes and colors, lined up in a row, with a stack of paper cups in front of each.

"We're down to deciding between these two," Ruby says, pointing to a tall cylindrical blue bottle and a smaller, pear-shaped pink bottle. "Do a taste test, will you, Willa?" Ruby says.

"What for?" I say.

"Mommy has to decide on what water to serve our clients at the spa."

"Isn't the spa for dogs?"

"Yes," Ruby says, fixing a stray red hair in the large, gold-framed mirror. Her fluffy dog, Pookie, runs over. "Hi, baby." Ruby picks up Pookie and kisses him on the lips. "All the top poochie spas have designer water. Mommies and daddies want the best for their babies, right, Pookie?" She rubs noses with the dog and kisses him again.

"This one is ten dollars a bottle," Tina says, tapping the pink one. "And this one is twenty." She holds up the pink bottle to show me. "Isn't it pretty?"

"Twenty dollars?" I say. "For a bottle of water? I'm sorry, but I think that's disgusting."

Tina and Ruby look at me, shocked. Pookie whimpers. Ruby holds Pookie tighter to her chest and covers his delicate ears.

"Think of what you could do with twenty dollars," I say. "You could probably feed a family for a day, *human beings*, and you're thinking of serving twenty-dollar-a-bottle water to dogs. *Dogs?*"

"*Ugh*," Ruby says, looking at me with utter disgust.

"What's wrong with you, Willa?" Tina says angrily.

"Nothing. I'm sorry. I've got to go."

I bike to the water, heart pounding, head spinning. How could Tina be changing so quickly? Every day she seems more like a clone of Ruby. I need to take a walk.

There aren't many people on the beach. *Good.* It's cloudy, looks like rain. I toss off my sandals, head out to the Spit, breathing in and out, in and out, letting the wind wash it all away. When I reach the tip, I stand still for a second and close my eyes. When I open them, I see a dog swimming out of the ocean toward me. I look around me. No one else is here.

The dog reaches the shore, shakes off water. It's the same dog I saw here with Mom and Sam yesterday. A big golden retriever . . . or, is it a Lab? . . . or, Irish setter? I don't know, I'm not a dog person.

The dog runs toward me like it knows me. I'm scared. What if it bites? . . . Then the dog tackles me on the sand and before I can catch my breath, this big fishy-smelling fur coat of a dog is licking my face, like he's kissing me, like I'm his long-lost owner who, at last, thank goodness, he's finally found.

Saltwater is dripping all over my face and all I can do is laugh.

CHAPTER 11

A Mermaid Gift

'*Twas one of the charmed days. . . .*
— Ralph Waldo Emerson

The dog is licking my cheeks, my nose, my eyebrows. It tickles. I'm laughing. "Whoa, whoa! Wait a minute. Stop. Who are you? What's your name?" I reach my hands around his neck. There just might be a collar in there somewhere. No, just handfuls of soft, smelly fur, so thick my hands could get lost in there. He's a big stinky polar bear.

"Come on, boy, let me up." I push the bear-dog away and stand up, wiping saliva off my face and brushing the sand off my back as best I can.

The dog is staring at me. He barks, "*Rrrr, rrrr, rrrr, rrrr,*" and wags his tail, "*rrrr, rrrr, rrrr, rrrr,*" like he's trying to tell me something.

Which most likely he is, if only I knew his language.

"Good dog, good dog," I say, rubbing my hands

down his coat. His fur is a rich golden color with a reddish tint. His eyes are big chocolate circles. His nose is wet. He opens his mouth wide, like he's showing me his teeth, and I worry, because isn't that a threatening gesture, but no, wait, he's smiling at me. *This dog is smiling at me.* My heart melts like an ice cream cone in the Cape Cod sun.

"Where's your owner, buddy?" I look all around, up and down the Spit.

There's a boat anchored a bit offshore, but I don't see anyone on it.

"Who do you belong to, huh?" I walk up over the dune.

The dog follows me. No one on the bay side, either.

I cross back over to the ocean side. The sun breaks through the clouds. Maybe it will be a nice day after all. The dog trots toward the cages where the plover nests are.

"No, buddy," I say in a loud, stern voice, "come here."

I whistle and slap my hand against my thigh like I've seen dog owners do. "Come here, boy." At least I think he's a boy, but I'm certainly not going to investigate.

The dog raises his head up above the sea grass and runs back to me.

"Good dog."

I start back down the beach. Maybe the owner is up in the beach parking lot. At first the dog doesn't move, but then he barks and comes running toward me. I rub his head as a reward. "Good dog, good dog."

He follows behind me for a few steps, and then comes up next to me so we're walking side by side. His fur brushes against my leg and I smile. What a nice dog.

Up ahead, I see Mariel bounding down the stairs with a beach towel, ready for a swim.

"Hi, Willa! Who's that? Did you get a *dog*?"

"No. I found him out on the Spit. He came swimming right out of the water. I didn't see an owner. He doesn't have a collar, either."

"Then he's for *you*!" Mare says.

I laugh. "No, I'm sure he belongs to someone. He's such a beautiful dog."

"Was there anyone else on the beach?" Mare asks.

"No, just me."

"Then the sea carried him to you," Mare says with great certainty. "My mother once told me that if you find a treasure on the beach first thing in the morning and you are the only human being in sight, then it is a gift to you from the mermaids."

I think about how Mare found the snorkel and goggles and how she thought it was a gift, but I don't say anything. I know how much Mare misses her mother. There's no sense debating the silliness of the mermaid idea. Dogs don't just wash up onshore like beach glass or jingle shells or snorkeling gear.

"I'm headed to my grandmother's store," I say. "Have a good swim."

"Thanks," Mare says. "Hey, Willa, maybe we can hang together later?"

"Sure," I say. "Why don't you come for dinner, say around six?"

"Sounds good." Mare takes off.

The dog sits at my feet, looking up at me, panting, like, "So, where are we off to now?"

I pat his head, lean down, and stroke his coat. "You stay here, buddy, okay? I've got to go. I'm sure your owner will be back soon."

It's strange, but I almost want to hug this dog. I think for a second, *I wish I could keep him*, but no way would my mother ever agree to that.

I get on my bike and pedal off quickly.

I hear the dog barking behind me, but I'm too sad to look back.

CHAPTER 12

No Buts About It

One man's justice is another's injustice;
one man's beauty another's ugliness;
one man's wisdom another's folly.
— Ralph Waldo Emerson

I bike into town, feeling bad about the dog. I look back a few times, but he's not following me. *Good.* I hope that means his owner found him. When I pass the ivy-covered Bramble Library, a breeze blows and the little green hands wave *hello, Willa, hello.* I love that old library.

I actually helped save it from closing down. My class hosted fund-raising dances in the barn at the inn. The dances were mine and Tina's idea. Our friends, Jessie and Luke, and their band performed. It was fun. The dances didn't raise much money at all, but two of our guests, the Blazers, had a ball at the Thanksgiving dance, which we named the "Turkey Tango," and when they got wind of the library situation and how much it meant to me, lo and behold, at our next dance, they became the library's very generous Valentine's donor. That was the night JFK and I danced in the barn by firelight and he gave me the heart-shaped locket.

I need to talk with him. Where has he been?

I pass the movie theater, the two-for-one tourist T-shirt shop, Fancy's Fish Market, and Wickstrom's Jewelers, where JFK bought the locket. If he doesn't call me back today, I'm biking over to his house tonight.

My hairdresser, Jo, is in the window of her salon, Hairs to You. There are tall silver buckets of pink-and-white stargazer lilies out in front of Delilah's Florist. I can't resist. I stop and breathe them in. *Hmmm, beautiful.*

When I get to Sweet Bramble Books, the bells above the door jangle a greeting, and the smell of chocolate, mint, and taffy swirl up to my nose, *hello.* Nana is at the counter weighing individual cellophane bags of penny candy for a family with several children. The father is watching the numbers on the scale and the mother is searching for something in her pocketbook. One of the kids, he looks about three years old, backs over to the gummy fish bin, checking to make sure his parents are still distracted, and then, with this big grin on his face, is just about to stick his hand in the fish when Nana calls out, without even looking, "Use the scoop, young man. Thank you."

The kid jumps, nearly pees his pants scared, like, *How did she see me?* I giggle quietly. Nana's got X-ray vision when it comes to kids messing with her gummy fish bin. Nana looks over at me and waves. Her dog, Scamp, comes to greet me. I bend down and scratch him around his ears like he likes, but instead of rolling on his back, so I can rub his belly, Scamp barks and sniffs my fingers. He probably smells the dog from the beach. I hope the dog found his owner by now.

Over on the book side of the store, Dr. Swaminathan, my English teacher at Bramble Academy, is just finishing with a customer. He's going to be working here part-time this summer. Nana said she's sure glad to have someone so highly knowledgeable about books. Nana is the candy expert. Gramp was the book lover in the family. He owned the town bookstore and then when he and Nana married, they combined their businesses into Sweet Bramble Books, my notion of the perfect store. Give me books and candy and I'm a happy camper.

"If you enjoy the book, there's a sequel due out in January," Dr. Swammy says to the customer. "Let me know what you think, Mrs. Goodale. I'll be interested to hear."

The lady thanks him and leaves.

It feels strange to see another man standing there behind the counter in my grandfather's spot, in the bookstore Gramp loved so much. I can feel Gramp's spirit here. I hope I always will. And I know Gramp would approve of Dr. Swaminathan. Dr. Swammy loves books the way Gramp loved books. Nana and I joke that Gramp's probably up in heaven right now, starting book clubs and making sure God reads the "good ones."

"Hello, Willa," Dr. Swammy says. "How's your summer going?"

"Great," I say. "Welcome back. How was India?"

"I enjoyed spending time with my family," he says, "but I was saddened by the spread of the water crisis."

"The water crisis?"

Dr. Swaminathan shakes his head. "Very, very dirty water."

I lean on the counter and Dr. Swammy explains how waterborne diseases are threatening the lives of thousands, maybe millions of people.

"The Ganges is poisoned," he says, "and yet people still drink from it. They scoop it up in their hands like you and I turn on a faucet in our kitchen. And the problem doesn't end there. The polluted water is also used for crops and so it affects the food supply as well. All across India," he says sadly. "Wells are closed, pumps are locked. People are dying of thirst."

People are dying because they don't have water. In this day and age? How can that be? I remember Sulamina Mum's words. "What can I do?" I say, ready to help.

Dr. Swammy smiles. He tells me about an organization he's affiliated with that raises money to bring in water treatment equipment and dig for new wells. As he talks, I think maybe I've found my new service project for the summer. I think about the fancy water bottles we have at the inn and the designer water at the pet spa. Something's very wrong with this picture. I decide to investigate this issue further online later.

Dr. Swaminathan asks what I'm reading.

"I haven't started our required class list yet," I say, "but don't worry, I'll get to it in August."

Dr. Swammy laughs. "I wasn't worried at all."

I tell Dr. Swammy about the skinny-punch books and some of the titles Mrs. Saperstone suggested for me.

"Very nice selections," Dr. Swaminathan says. He stares at me for a second. "Willa, do you know . . . is Mrs. Saperstone staying in Bramble for the summer?"

There's an unfamiliar sweetness in the tone of Dr. Swammy's voice. I look at him and he looks away, as if embarrassed.

"I want to consult with her about a writing contest I'm thinking of starting," he says, not looking at me while he's talking.

Beep-beep-beep. My Cape-cupid radar goes off in my brain. Dr. Swammy likes Mrs. Saperstone! Of course. I've seen them sitting together at BUC. They'd be perfect for each other. They're both single, about the same age, and they both love books. *Perfect.*

If I may brag for a moment, I do have a stellar reputation for matchmaking. First, I hooked up my mother and Sam. I should have won a gold medal for that one. Even though Stella Havisham had a booming business planning other people's weddings, my mother had written off love for herself. She had been so brokenhearted over my father's death. It took a long time, but it was worth the wait.

Next, I played cupid for Nana and Gramp Tweed. He ran a bookstore; she ran Clancy's Candies. Books and candy, my two favorite things. Nana and Mr. Tweed, my two favorite people. It was a no-brainer, truly. I invited them to a picnic at my house and *boing*, it was love at first bite (of the picnic food, I mean, no vampires in Bramble that I know of).

My most recent match was Sulamina Mum and Riley Truth. All I did was coax Mum into writing a letter to her long-lost high school sweetheart — it was no easy task, she fought me on it — but, finally, Mum took a leapfrog leap of faith and wrote Riley a letter and *boing*, that letter hit home better than that bare-butt baby's bow and arrow. I'm now a firm believer in being a "leaper." Sometimes you've just got to close your eyes and leap right over the scary part, to get to the thing you want.

"You should go to the Bramble Library tonight," I say. "Mrs. Saperstone is doing a program on good 'beach reads.' The Red Hat ladies were talking about it this —"

"The Red Hat whos?"

"This cool group of ladies who are staying at the inn. But, enough about them. Back to Mrs. Saperstone. It starts at seven. There'll be iced tea and refreshments. I know she'd love to see you."

"Really?" Dr. Swaminathan says.

I can't tell for sure, but he looks like he's blushing.

"Absolutely." I nod my head definitively. "Oh, and, maybe you'd like to bring her some candy? I know Mrs. Saperstone loves those chocolate-covered cranberries Nana makes."

Back over on the candy side of Sweet Bramble Books, Nana comes toward me with her arms wide open. "Give me a hug, shmug."

I tell Nana what I found out about the new salt-water taffy section at Ghelfi's. "You can't compete with their variety," I say, "so we need a different strategy."

"Okay, good," Nana says, looking around the store for spies, rubbing her hands together, lowering her voice to a whisper. "Hit me with it."

"I was thinking . . . you know how you get those little messages inside fortune cookies and how much fun that can be?"

Nana nods her head yes.

"Well, what if we tied happy thoughts around the taffies, like they do around Hershey's Kisses. Sort of add to the value of the purchase? Create a new candy buzz?"

Nana claps her hands, all excited. "I like it!"

"I can write the messages," I say, "no problem. All you'd need to do is print them out and cut and —"

"Brilliant!" Nana says, hugging me. "I tell you, Willa Havisham Gracemore, you've got good candy genes. Good book sense and candy smarts. Sweet Bramble Books will be yours someday."

Outside, I get on my bike, feeling proud that I can help Nana. I'll start writing those taffy tags today. It'll be fun.

Passing the town green, I spot the dog from the beach. He looks up at me and barks and runs toward me like he's been waiting for me. I keep biking.

He's following me.

I turn the corner toward home and sure enough, the dog follows me up the driveway to the Bramblebriar Inn. I can hear him panting behind me.

Maybe if I ignore him, he'll go away.

"Willa! Come say hello," my mother calls to me. She's sitting on the front porch with Katie Caldor, Mrs. Caldor, and four pretty girls, probably Katie's bridesmaids, most likely going over last-minute wedding details.

Mrs. Caldor is wearing a stunning pale blue sundress with a matching hat. The Caldors are known for exquisite taste in fashion. They own the chain of Caldor Creek clothing stores that started right here on Cape Cod.

I start up the steps. I hear the dog following me.

Go. Go away.

"What a cute dog!" Katie Caldor says, and as if on cue, the dog bounds up to the wicker table, knocking over the pitcher of lemonade right onto Mrs. Caldor's lap.

She jumps up, horrified.

"Oh, Vivian, I'm so sorry," my mother says, peeling a lemon rind off of Mrs. Caldor's beautiful dress. "Willa, run and get a towel and some club soda."

After the Caldors leave, I bring the dog a dish of water. He laps it up gratefully and then sprawls out under a shady tree, big brown eyes looking up sheepishly.

"That's the dog that defecated on the beach yesterday, isn't it?" Stella says.

"Mom, give him a break. He's just a dog." And then, I know she'll say no but I always say you've got to be a leaper and so I take a leap: "Mom, do you think he could stay here for a while until we find the owner? I'll make up signs and post them around town. . . ."

"Absolutely not," she says. "In fact, please go ask

Sam to call animal control or town hall or whomever one calls about these things."

"Mom, that's not fair."

My mother lowers her voice as some guests walk by. "You heard me, Willa."

"But, Mom . . ."

"No buts about it, Willa. I don't want a dog traipsing through my inn."

My temper flares. "Well, it's my home, too, and you better get ready for no *mutts* about it, because the Sivlers are opening up a pampered pet spa next door and *dogs* are going to be our new neighbors."

CHAPTER 13

Salty from the Sea

Nothing great was ever achieved without enthusiasm.
— Ralph Waldo Emerson

I storm into the inn to look for Sam. He's out in the vegetable garden.

His eyes smile when he sees me. Sam is always happy to see me.

I burst into tears and tell him what's going on.

"Well," Sam says, taking off his gloves, "first let's see this dog."

We walk out front to the big oak tree. The dog is sound asleep. Sam kneels on the grass beside him and gently pets the dog. The dog opens his eyes. He looks at Sam and then he looks at me.

I pet him and he licks my hand.

"What a gorgeous golden," Sam says.

"So he's a golden retriever?"

"Yep. I had one, growing up."

"What was your dog's name, Dad?"

"Henry."

I laugh. "Where did you get the name Henry?"

"I don't know," Sam says, laughing, "but I'm sure it made perfect sense at the time." Sam rubs his hands through fur. The dog rolls on his back and lifts up his paw like he wants to shake Sam's hand. Sam shakes his paw and laughs, "Good dog."

"What happened to Henry?" I ask.

"He died of old age when I was in college. He lived a good, long life, though, old Henry did. Ruthie and I . . . we loved that dog."

"Speaking of Aunt Ruthie," I say, "I think I've got everything planned for the wedding." I tell Sam my idea to hold the ceremony in the Labyrinth. It seems only fitting that Sam's sister should say "I do" there. The Labyrinth is Sam's creation. It's a circular garden path. You enter between two shrubs and follow the narrow walkway, looping in toward the center, out toward the border, circling around and around until you reach the stone bench in the middle. Sam says walking the Labyrinth is a spiritual thing for him. Sam has planted perennial flowers and berried bushes all along the borders so that there's always something beautiful blooming as you walk. It's funny, though, when I walk the Labyrinth, I don't focus on the flowers at all. I walk and breathe and wait to hear whatever comes up inside me.

My mother comes down the steps to join us. "Have you reported this yet?"

Sam turns and looks at my mother. She folds her arms across her chest.

"I was just about to do that, Stella," Sam says, turning back to the dog and scratching behind his ears. "Such a beautiful dog."

"Shake my hand, boy," I say, and sure enough he does.

"What a smart dog!" I say. I look at my mother. She isn't melting a bit.

"Oh, and watch this, Mom," I say. "He *smiles*." I smile a great big jack-o'-lantern toothy smile at the dog. "Come on, buddy, smile. Smile."

The dog looks at my mother and barks.

"Well, if you aren't going to call someone, I will," Mom says. "This dog could have fleas or ticks or rabies or who knows what." She walks up the stairs and into the inn.

Sam leaves. "Be right back."

I stay with my dog from the sea. I have the strange sense again that someone is watching me. I look up quickly at that second-floor window next door. But, no, nothing. I shake it off.

Sam returns with some leftovers from last night's dinner. The dog sniffs the roast beef and turns away.

"I think he prefers seafood," I say.

Sam goes in and comes back with a bowl of dry cereal. This is more to the dog's liking. The Millers are walking up the driveway. They come over to see the dog. Mike the mailman comes and I go to get our mail. Two postcards for me! One from Mum and Riley from Disney World. One from Suzanna Jubilee and Simon on their honeymoon in Italy. "Venice is spectacular," Suzie writes. "We ride the gondolas every day. And you should see the boys here, Willa. Bellissimo, Bellissimo. We're coming to visit you in August! I'll bring pictures. Ciao, bella bebe, hugs and kisses, Suzie Jube."

Mum writes, "We met Mickey and Minnie, took a ride in Cindy's pumpkin, and had breakfast with Pooh. The fireworks show was spectacular, but couldn't hold a sparkler to Cape fireworks on the Fourth of July. I miss Bramble. Hope you like the new minister. Give my love to everyone. And please tell Stella and Sam to plan a visit. Riley and I would love to show you some Southern hospitality. Love, Mum."

There's a letter addressed to the Bramblebriar Inn, "Attention Rosie." I note the return address. It's from Mrs. Chickles Blazer at the Blazers' California zip code. They own at least three mansions in this country and a château in Paris, too.

Hmmmm. I wonder why Mama B is writing to Rosie? It must be about the wedding cake. At Suzie Jube's wedding Mama B nearly split a seam raving about that wedding cake. She said it was the best she'd ever eaten. "Give me your phone number, honey. Papa B and I are going to make you famous!"

The animal control truck pulls up. A man in a gray uniform gets out, says his name is Mark Sweeney. He asks me where I found the dog. I tell him as much as I can recall. Mr. Sweeney approaches the dog slowly and gently puts a harness around him.

"Where are you taking him?" I ask, feeling like I'm going to cry.

"Bramble Animal Shelter."

"Where's that?"

"On Mill Road, across from the waste treatment plant," he says, then laughs. "Not much of a location, but we just planted some flowers out front."

I know where the waste treatment plant is. It's on the way to Mariel's.

"What are you going to do with him?" I ask in a very stern voice, like, *You better treat him well.*

Sam comes over next to me and puts his hand on my shoulder. My mother goes in the house.

"We'll scan him for a chip," Mr. Sweeney says. He explains that many pet owners now have a microchip implanted in their dogs and cats for easy identification if they get lost.

"We'll check him for fleas, give him a bath. This one's a smelly guy, huh, boy?"

"He's just salty from the sea," I say, defending my dog.

"We'll give him a rabies shot. Check him over. Be sure he's not injured. If he is, we'll bring him to the vet; otherwise, we'll just kennel him and hold him for five days."

"How do you try to find the owner?" Sam asks.

"We'll post a photo on our Web site and hope for a call."

"What happens after five days?" I say, all worried. What if they put him to sleep?

"It's Bramble town policy, after the fifth day, if the owner doesn't show, we get the animal ready for adoption. We'll make sure he's neutered, flea-free, run him through a behavioral test, and then put him up for adoption."

"*Adoption?*" I say. I look at Sam. He nods and smiles reassuringly.

I feel hope rising inside me like a balloon. "You mean if no one comes in a week, we could adopt him?"

"Sure," Mr. Sweeney says. "And I hope you will. You'd have to pay a fee, of course, and we'd have to come do a home inspection, a background check . . ."

"A background check?" Sam says.

"Well, basically, we'd talk with your neighbors and make sure there's no history of animal cruelty."

"We love animals," I say, already auditioning for the role of "Mom." "And there's a pet spa opening right next door, so you can be sure he would be pampered."

"Well, that sounds fine," Mr. Sweeney says, "but for now, I've got to take this guy in. See if his owners show up."

My eyes fill with tears. *Don't show up, don't show up. This is my dog now.* I hug Salty Dog and whisper, "Don't worry, boy, you'll be okay. I'll come visit you tomorrow."

Up in my room, I take out my journal and pour out fast what's happening.

I might adopt a dog! He's already mine. In my heart, I know he is. Mare's right. He came to me. From the mermaids, straight out of the sea.

I think about that boat anchored in the bay.

Could Salty—that's what I'd name him—have fallen overboard? No. That would have been a very long way to swim. Dogs don't like to swim that far, right? I have no idea. I don't know much about dogs at all. Except that I love this one. Sam and I have a whole week to work on Mother. Maybe when she sees how much we both want . . .

When I finish writing, I take out my bag of salt-water taffy. I'm in the mood for peppermint. I open a smooth white-and-red striped candy and pop it in my mouth. That reminds me. The messages for Nana's "taffy tags." I like this idea. I should get a patent on it or something—I bet that's what Tina would tell me to do.

I wonder how Tina and Ruby's book is coming along.

I grab a notebook and pen. Let's see . . . taffy, taffy . . .

Eat Taffy. Be Happy.
A taffy a day keeps the troubles away.
One taffy's good; two is better.
Don't Worry. Be Taffy.

Sandy sneakers, taffy teeth — Welcome to Cape Cod.

I laugh and put the notebook aside. Nana's going to love these. Nana would be so happy for me if I could adopt Salty. Why does Stella have to be so mean?

I look at my short stack of skinny-punch books, scanning the titles. Which to choose next? *The Hundred Dresses* by Eleanor Estes, *The Whipping Boy* by Sid Fleischman. My eyes land on *Love that Dog* by Sharon Creech. I know that author. She won the Newbery Medal for *Walk Two Moons*. I open *Dog* and start reading.

When I get to the line about the "yellow dog," I smile.

I'm going to have a yellow dog, too.

Soon, I just know I will.

CHAPTER 14

Stupid Baseball

The only way to have a friend is to be one.
— Ralph Waldo Emerson

Mariel comes at six for dinner. With her deep brown eyes, glistening skin, and long black ringlety hair, she's stunning in a simple jean skirt and tank top. She has on the beach-glass necklace, with the blue-green-white-brown, blue-green-white-brown pattern she was wearing the day I discovered that she and Joseph were friends. We all ran into one another outside of Nana's store. It was awkward. I was jealous when she got the role of Emily in *Our Town* and JFK got the male lead and they kissed in the play, but JFK insisted that he and Mare were just friends.

"Am I too early?" Mare says.

"No, you're right on time. Come on in. My mom's out shopping and my dad's running the kitchen tonight, so it'll just be us."

I worked out the menu with Sam ahead of time. Barbecued chicken, potato salad, sliced tomatoes, and green beans.

"Hello, Mariel," Sam says, draining a pot at the sink and then moving back to the sizzling pan on the burner. "Welcome. How's your summer going?"

"Great, Mr. Gracemore, thanks."

"Can we expect to see you in any more productions this summer?" Sam asks.

"I want to audition for Maid Marian in *Robin Hood*," Mare says, "but the Wellfleet playhouse is out of biking distance, so we'll see."

That must be the audition she was talking to JFK about at the baseball field. I sure hope he's not auditioning. Aren't Robin Hood and Maid Marian in love? I'm certain there would be kissing.

Something steams up on the stove and Sam turns. "I'm sorry . . . back to work. Why don't you girls fill your plates and sit out at the picnic table by the pond? It's a perfect evening for alfresco dining. And I've got the wickets set up for croquet."

"That sounds nice," Mare says. "Thanks for having me over, Mr. Gracemore."

We fill our plates and head outside. I tell Mare to duck when we pass by the dining room window. "If the Red Hats spot us, they'll want to talk all night, or worse yet, join us."

Mare laughs. "I like them. I plan on being a Red Hat when I'm older. Red hat, red shoes, red everything. I want to live life *big* and have some fun. Don't you, Willa?"

"Absolutely."

We talk about the plover thing. We talk about books. Mare says she's reading *Esperanza Rising* by Pam Muñoz Ryan, and highly recommends it. I ask her how long it is. I tell her I'll try it when I'm off my diet. Mare laughs when I tell her about the skinny-punch books. She says she wants to try that, too.

"I'll give you my Willa's Pix list," I say.

"Where did you get that idea from?" she asks.

I tell her how I went to Saratoga, New York, with Tina and her family on a summer vacation and we visited the famous racetrack there. Local kids do a daily "Kid's Pix" listing their favorite horses in each of the races for that day. That seems like so long ago now. Something tells me that if Tina had to pick a friend to go with her this summer, she would pick Ruby.

I look at Mare. She's looking out at the pond, enjoying her food, enjoying being here. Such a different place from the ugly, cramped motel she lives in.

I'm glad Mare's here. I like her, a lot. I can tell we're going to be good friends, but right now I'm hoping she won't stay too long. I want to see JFK tonight.

"I can only hang out until seven," I say. "I hope that's okay." *She's your friend, Willa, just tell her the truth. No . . . what if she wants to come, too?*

"Oh, sure," Mare says. "I need to leave soon anyway. I promised Papa I'd pick up some things at the market."

"How is your father? And Nico and Sofia?"

Mariel's father is in a wheelchair. JFK said he was injured in a work-related accident. I'm not sure how. Nico and Sofia are twins, three years old, I think. I don't ask Mare about her mother. I want to, but it feels too personal. I'm hoping she'll talk about her someday, though. JFK said Mrs. Sanchez is an actress off pursuing her "big break," with Mariel's blessing, if you can believe it. Mare told JFK her mother was like a bird who would die if her wings were clipped. Well, that might be so, but it seems to me a mother bird shouldn't fly off and leave her babies, no matter how talented she is.

We bring our dishes into the kitchen. Sam gives Mare a container of fresh-from-the-oven chocolate chip cookies to bring home to her family. When Mare leaves, I go upstairs and fix my hair, brush my teeth, and put on some lip gloss and perfume. I put some cookies in a bag, stick it in the basket of my bike, and head toward JFK's, taking a different route so I won't run into Mariel passing by the market.

As I pass the gray clapboard Bramble Beach Association building, the parking lot is full. A sign reads: IMPORTANT MEETING TONIGHT. 7 PM.

That's funny, I don't remember Mom and Sam talking about a meeting tonight. We belong to the BBA. All the people who own homes in this area do, a couple hundred families I think it is. We pay yearly dues for beach maintenance and landscaping and other stuff. In the summer, there are softball games, craft classes, and movies for kids, and card games and things for adults. Nana likes the Thursday night square dances. The big event is the Fourth of July Field Day, coming up next week.

I wonder what the meeting's about? I wheel my bike into the rack and go inside.

Ruby Sivler's father is at the front of the room. There's Tina's father, Mr. Belle. There's the lady who owns the huge white house with the swimming pool right at the entrance to Sandy Beach. Several people I recognize as Ruby and Tina's neighbors. The "boat crowd" as Sam would say.

"It's high time we took back our beach," Mr. Sivler is saying. "First we've got intruders trespassing on our beach, more and more each summer, and now the best part of the Spit is roped off for *birds*. I don't know about you, but I work hard all week. I want to enjoy my beach on the weekends. There's something wrong with this picture, people."

There's lots of clapping.

"We need to protect our investment," Tina's father, Mr. Belle, says. "And we need to take action, quickly. The sand on the Spit is slipping away like the proverbial hourglass. First it's a few beach towels and a boat anchored here and there, next thing you know, they'll be pitching tents and acting like they live here."

There's a commotion throughout the room.

"As president of the BBA," Mr. Sivler says, "I've taken the liberty of developing a system for preserving our rights and policing what we're entitled to."

Mr. Sivler explains that every Bramble family who has "legal deeded rights" to the beach will be given a small white flag with a number on it. He holds one up and waves it to show how simple the idea is. "Each certified BBA member family whose annual dues are paid will be assigned a flag with a number. "When you're at the beach, just post your flag in the sand next to you. Then we'll all know who belongs here and who doesn't."

"How we gonna enforce that?" someone shouts out.

"Good question," Mr. Sivler says. "We've hired three retired police officers to patrol the beach and guard the entrances to the parking lot. They will approach unfamiliar people and ask to see their flag. If the party cannot produce a flag, they will be escorted off the beach."

There's a rumble of *good*s and *that's right*s and lots of heads nodding.

I feel uneasy inside. Something's not right here.

"But this system will only work if we all participate," Mr. Sivler says. "We must be vigilant. If you are on the beach and see a party you don't recognize, ask them to produce their flag. Or, if you are uncomfortable approaching strangers, which is perfectly understandable in the world we live in today, just talk to one of the patrol officers and they'll take care of the situation."

"The bottom line is this," the lady who hires the lifeguards says, "you either belong on this beach or you don't. We're just protecting what's ours."

You've got to be kidding me. They sound like a bunch of toddlers crying, "Stay away from my sandbox or I'm going to tell my mommy!" Maybe that's why Tina was asking Mariel who she was with on the beach, implying that she didn't belong there. Mariel bikes miles from her crummy motel-room home to swim at this beach. She's not harming anything. I think the flag thing is a stupid idea and I have half a mind to speak my piece about the beach, but it will be dark soon and I've got my priorities in order. Boyfriend? Beach? Boyfriend? Beach? That's easy.

When I get to Joseph's house, there he is, sitting on the steps talking to Mariel. *What is she doing here?* I drop my bike on the lawn and walk toward them.

"Hey, Willa," Mariel says, standing up to go. "Well, I better go — I have to pick up milk. See ya later, Joe. Sorry you can't do *Robin Hood*, but I'm happy for you. Have fun. Send me a postcard, okay? See you guys later."

I don't say anything to Mariel as she leaves. I'm not sure whether to be suspicious or jealous or what. I walk up the stairs.

JFK smiles and says, "Hi."

"Where have you been?" I say. "Why haven't you called? I've left you tons of messages."

"I know, Willa. I'm sorry. Stuff came up. . . ."

"What stuff?" I'm angry. *What stuff could be more important than your girlfriend?*

"Baseball."

Of course.

"Guess what," he says, all excited. "My dad's friend, the sports editor down at the paper, got me a gig working at the Miami Dolphins training camp!"

"In *Florida*?"

"Yes! Isn't that cool? I can stay with my grandparents and . . ."

"When?" I say, my heart sinking into my stomach.

"I'm leaving Friday, I think. As soon as Dad gets my ticket and Mom finishes packing me up." His face is glowing.

"For how long?"

"The whole month."

"Wow," I say, "that's great."

"I know," JFK says. "Can you believe it!"

"No," I say, looking away.

"Listen . . . Willa," JFK says. "I'm sorry I got down on you for not telling me you were scared the other day. I just think we should trust each other enough to tell the truth."

I have very good taste in boyfriends. I smile. "Were you really considering another play with Mariel?" There, I got it out.

"Maybe." JFK smiles. "Don't tell me you're jealous? Come on." He hugs me.

We talk for a while, about small stuff. He's so happy, I don't tell him how I truly feel. First, I spoiled his joy about the sailboat. I'm not going to rain on his baseball parade, too. *It's only a month. Deal with it, Willa. But it's summer vacation and he's my boyfriend. Right, but he's your friend, too. See how happy he is? Be happy for him. He'd be happy for you. Stupid baseball. Soccer is a much better sport.*

"It's dark," Joseph says, "I'll bike you home."

When we get to the inn, all the lights are lit up and someone's playing the piano. Next door, the soon-to-be pet spa is all lit up, too, except that one upstairs window. Several workers are inside, hanging curtains, opening boxes, filling shelves. There's a sign out front: GRAND OPENING JULY 1ST. That's this Saturday. My first solo wedding day. And I wanted JFK to come. I try not to be upset.

We sit up on the old stone fence. JFK inches in closer to me. Crickets are chirping, a firefly flits past, the sky is brimming with stars. *Stop showing off, Nature.*

Joseph takes my hand, twines his fingers through mine. "Hey," he says in a sweet, soft voice. "Why so quiet?"

"No reason."

He touches my chin, turns it toward him, and then he kisses me. He smells faintly of sunscreen; he was probably sailing today. We kiss until I hear the Red Hats laughing and hollering and hooting it up as they walk up the street from town. Those ladies are having way too much fun just coming from the library. Their laughter is contagious. It makes us laugh, too.

"I'll call you tomorrow," JFK says. He jumps down from the fence and then reaches his hands around my waist to help me down. We kiss again. So what if the Red Hats see!

I'm too wired to write in my journal. My mind is spinning. I can't sleep. I go up on the widow's walk. Long ago, Cape Cod wives would pace back and forth on these rooftop perches, staring out to sea, hoping to spot their husband's boat sailing safely home to harbor. Unfortunately, the whaling life was a treacherous one, and many men died at sea. Thus the name "widow's walk." I check out the sky, spot the North Star and the Dippers, let the air *whoosh* against my face, then go back to my room, still restless.

I reach for *Locomotion* by Jacqueline Woodson. There are three books by her in my summer stack. I pull out my taffy and start reading:

This whole book's a poem 'cause every time I try to tell the whole story my mind goes Be quiet! . . .

The taffy wrappers pile up. I finish the book in an hour. Wow, can this lady write. I love "the voice." English teacher Sam says you can teach people a lot of things about writing — plotting, pacing, characterization — but voice, that's something of a mystery. Sam says a writer either has it or she doesn't. Jacqueline Woodson has it.

When I snuggle under the covers, I close my eyes and the movie starts in my mind. JFK and I kissing on the old stone fence. At least we have four more days before he leaves. At least he's not heading out to sea for who knows how long on a whale hunt. Stupid baseball. Then I picture Salty Dog smiling at me and wonder how he's doing.

CHAPTER 15

Bad, Bad Bottle

*Beware when the great God lets loose
a thinker on this planet.*

— Ralph Waldo Emerson

When I finish work Tuesday morning, I bike fast as I can to Mill Road, holding my breath as I pass the garbage treatment plant. Gosh, does that place stink.

There are red, white, and blue petunias planted in a flag pattern outside of Bramble Animal Shelter. Mr. Sweeney smiles when he sees me.

"I had a feeling I'd be seeing you today," he says.

"Did the owner come?" I ask, heart pounding. *Please, please, say no.*

"No," he says, smiling. "Want to see him?"

"Yes!" I follow Mr. Sweeney back into the kennel area. We walk past a row of cats who peer sadly and quietly out at me, then into the dog section where they jump and pace and bark, making a ruckus to get my attention. I look at each animal as we pass, smiling and silently saying, *Don't worry, stay hopeful, some-one will adopt you, I'm sure.* And then I see my dog.

"Salty!"

Mr. Sweeney unlocks the cage. Salty jumps toward me. I kneel and hug him tight. He smells different, like soap. "So you got a bath, huh, boy?"

Mr. Sweeney gives me some treats for Salty and lets me take him out on a leash in the backyard. Salty seems so happy to see me. I stay for an hour. I hug him tight and look straight in his eyes. "Don't forget me, Salty."

He smiles and barks.

"Be back tomorrow, bye!"

I'm over in Mariel's neighborhood. Maybe she's home. I bike past the trailer park, then I see the sign OCEANVIEW INN: TOURISTS WELCOME.

The Oceanview Inn is a dirty, dumpy, run-down motel that hasn't welcomed a tourist in a long time. It's an inch up from a homeless shelter, yards down from an apartment building, miles away from being a real house.

Poor people who can't afford the cost of an apartment here on Cape Cod rent rooms here by the month. Mariel's whole family lives in one room, Room #5.

Two people are arguing loudly in #7, a baby's crying in #6. As I approach the Sanchez's door, I hear singing. It's a young woman's voice, must be Mariel. The melody is familiar, but the words are in Spanish and I'm not sure. What a beautiful voice.

I stand there listening for a moment. When I knock, the singing stops.

I hear little-kid giggling, Nico and Sofia, and then Mare opens the door.

"Willa!" She seems confused and embarrassed. She moves me outside, closing the door behind us. I can hear the twins giggling louder, like this is some sort of game.

"What are you doing here?" Mare says, not in a happy tone.

"I was in the neighborhood and I thought I'd stop by."

"Why didn't you call first?" she says.

"I'm sorry." But inside I'm thinking, *You've stopped by my house without calling first.*

"What are you doing around here?" she asks.

"The animal shelter up the road," I say. "I went to visit the dog I found."

"*Your dog*," Mare says, her face brightening.

"I hope so," I say.

"No, he's yours," Mare says, confident as one of

those court judges on TV. "I told you, it is a gift from the mermaids."

"What are you doing today?" I say, trying to change the subject. I feel sort of hurt that she isn't inviting me in.

"I have to watch the kids. My dad's working."

"I'd like to meet them," I say.

Mare stares at me for a second like she's considering this.

"What's wrong?" I say.

"It's just that they get all excited about meeting new people and then they keep asking when they're going to see them again."

"Well, no problem there," I say. "I think they'll be seeing a lot of me."

Mare smiles. I smile back. We don't say it, but I know we're both thinking the same thing: We're going to be good friends. Her brother and sister will see me again.

When Mare opens the door, Sofia and Nico are hiding under the bed. "Ooh, where have those little kittens gone," Mare says, and we hear the giggling. "Meow, meow, meow," they say, crawling out. Mare introduces us. We have animal crackers and apple juice. We play Candy Land, my favorite game when I was their age. When I tell Nico and Sofia that my grandmother owns a candy store, their eyes bug large like I'm a rock star on MTV.

"I'll bring you some candy next time I come. What kind do you like?"

"Bring it all!" Nico says.

"*Mucho, mucho*," Sofia says, and they roll on the floor giggling.

When I get home, I go up to my room and look over the plans for Ruthie's wedding. The weather is supposed to be nice on Saturday. We'll do the ceremony in the Labyrinth. There will only be twenty or so guests, and the service will be short, so we can all stand in a circle around Ruthie and Spruce. I think they should sit on the stone bench in the center. Yes, we'll all be there in the inner circle while they process in through the Labyrinth. Sam helped me pick some readings and Ruthie's favorite poem. It's the one by Robert Frost about "the road less traveled." I'm still not sure about music. When we hold formal wedding ceremonies at BUC, Mrs. Bellimo belts out songs from the choir loft. We can't do that in the Labyrinth. I ask Sam. He says you can't go wrong with the Beatles. He gives me some

CDs. I pick out "Here Comes the Sun" and "Let It Be" and "Imagine." Now I just need to find someone to sing them. I think of Mariel singing this morning. I wonder if she'd be willing?

JFK calls and asks if I want to bike out to Woods Hole.

"I'll pack lunch," I say. Tuna fish sandwiches and Cape Cod chips, peaches, brownies, and two bottled waters.

We take the Shining Sea bike trail out to Woods Hole, through a shady treed area with lots of wildflowers, out along a beautiful strip of the coastline, past Nobska Lighthouse standing tall.

Woods Hole is a cool town. Scientists from all over the world come here to conduct ocean research. We lock our bikes on a rack in the center park area and walk through town. They're feeding the harbor seals at the research aquarium at the end of the street. I remember Nana taking me here during summers when I was little and would come to stay with her while Mom was busy with her wedding planning business. There's a "please touch" water box inside the building. I'll never forget the first time I picked up a live starfish, a horseshoe crab, and a lobster, all slimy and wriggling in my hand.

We walk back to the park, check out the old sundial in the center. JFK takes a long drink from the orange bottle with the black top he has hooked on his belt loop. We find a grassy spot in the shade and I take out our lunch.

"You should get a reusable water container," JFK says, holding up one of my "Only the best for Bramblebriar guests" bottles and turning it around in the sun. "These plastic bottles are wicked bad for the planet. I did a science project at my old school in Minnesota. Americans buy, like, thirty billion of these a year."

"At least they get recycled," I say.

"Actually, only about one-fifth of them do. The other eighty percent end up in landfills. The plastic never breaks down. It's awful for the earth and animals, especially birds. They ingest it and choke and die. Not to mention the oil."

"What do you mean?"

"I think I remember it takes something like fifty million gallons of oil a year to make these plastic bottles, just here in America alone. And then there's the carbon dioxide pollution made during the manu-facturing."

I have excellent taste in boyfriends if I do say so myself. Not only is Joseph handsome, kind, poetic, and smart, but he thinks about bigger issues like stopping the war and saving the planet. I hold up my bottle: Only the best for Bramblebriar Guests. "Bad, bad bottle," I say in a stern voice. JFK laughs. "No, seriously," I say, "I'm going to get a refillable bottle like yours, Joseph. Do they come in green?"

He laughs. "Yeah, they come in lots of colors."

"Mine will have to be green, for Bramblebriar, of course."

After lunch we get ice cream and sit with our legs dangling off the pier, watching the boats come in and out. I turn just as Joseph is pointing to something and his cone bumps into my nose. He wipes off the ice cream, then kisses my nose.

I feel like I'm going to cry. "I'm going to miss you."

He smiles so sweetly. "It's only a month, Willa. I won't forget you."

We bike home, wind sailing through my hair, sun beating on my face. It's a perfect date on a perfect summer day. Neither of us mentions Florida. Bad, bad baseball.

JFK has to go somewhere with his family. I bike into town to tell Nana about the taffy tags I've come up with so far. Dr. Swaminathan and Mrs. Saperstone are coming out of a restaurant. They are laughing, all happy about something. Dr. Swammy opens the door of his car and Mrs. S gets in, just as I'm pulling up behind them. I don't call out. "Let those young love-birds alone" is what Nana would say. Dr. Swammy has a bumper sticker: THINK GLOBAL. START LOCAL. I think about that for a minute.

Nana loves the taffy taglines. She writes them down. "I'll get these printed up right away," she says. I get some mints for Mom, chocolate walnut fudge for Sam, and me . . . I'm in the mood for fish. I "remember the scoop" and shovel up a bag of those yummy red gummy guppies.

Back at the inn, I help with the cocktail social hour. I cut veggies and scoop out fresh dill dip into a bowl. I light little yellow candles out on the sunporch, turn on some music, carry out the fresh fruit and cheese plat-ter, and mingle around, chatting with the guests.

The Red Hats are off to dinner at Wimpy's in Osterville and then karaoke night at the British American Brew Pub in Falmouth. They've been prac-ticing some songs all day. They show me their red boas and test out a few lines of a song from the musical

Chicago. Oh, I wish Chickles Blazer was here. Mama B would love these gals!

Up in my room, I check out my books. Tonight I'm in the mood for comedy. Mrs. S was surprised that I hadn't read *The Whipping Boy* by Sid Fleischman. Great illustration on the cover. I plop down on my bed, dig into the fish, and start reading.

Mrs. S was right. This is a hoot.

I brush my teeth, which are all red from the fish, and think about what I'm going to wear for Ruthie and Spruce's wedding. They're coming Thursday. No need for a rehearsal Friday; it will be such a simple affair. I look through my closet, not sure what to wear. I don't know how formal Ruthie's going to be. I pull out the dress I wore in Suzie Jube's wedding. It's pale yellow, the color of sherbet, silky, with a poofy skirt that swirled when I danced. I felt like a princess in this dress. I was Suzie's maid of honor. I try it on. Yep, still looks good. I hang it back up and pull out the dress I wore the following day for Mum and Riley's wedding. I was Mum's maid of honor, too. This is a simple linen sundress, pale pink. It looked so nice with my silver locket and little silver dangling earrings. I try on the dress. Yep, still good.

I pick up *The Hundred Dresses* by Eleanor Estes, written more than sixty years ago. I leaf through it before I start. There are black-and-white illustrations throughout with bursts of watercolor colors here and there. It's about a girl named Wanda who wears the same old dress to school every day, and is teased by the "in girls" who have many beautiful dresses. It's a quick read, a powerful story. Definitely a skinny-punch.

Enough books for today. Time for a movie. I change into my pajamas and shut off the light. As soon as my head hits the pillow, the summer matinee starts in my mind.

JFK and I bike along that sunny bike path, the wind whistling, boats bobbing in the water. He looks at me with those sea-blue eyes and kisses ice cream from my nose.

I wish JFK could see my first wedding. I wish we could dance all night.

CHAPTER 16

The Cape Cod Beach Boys

Art is a jealous mistress.

— Ralph Waldo Emerson

Wednesday sails by in a minute.

I visit Salty. Hoorah, still no owner.

I see Tina and Ruby as they are coming out of Cohen's card shop in town. Their "book" is "going to be a bestseller!"

"It's not all wordy like a lot of books," Tina says. "Just a little bio on each boy . . . places where they like to take dates, their taste in music . . . you know, just the important stuff."

So far, they've got twenty boys featured from four Cape towns and they're not stopping till they hit Provincetown. That's the final point on the Cape. After that, they'd have to head out onto the Atlantic, hunting for hunky fishermen. Which might actually not be a bad idea for a sequel.

"Wow, that sounds like a lot of work," I say.

"The price one pays for art," Ruby says, wiping her brow like she's been cleaning toilets all day. Tina giggles.

"Do you have a title yet?" I ask. Wait until I tell Mariel about this.

"*The Beach Boys of Cape Cod*," Tina says.

"I like it," I say.

"We're not sure about the price," Ruby says. "We're thinking fifty, sixty bucks."

"For a book?" I say.

"Well, it's words *and pictures*," Tina says. "And wait until you see these photographs. Ruby is a really good photographer. I mean, this is going to be like the summer swimsuit issue of *Sports Illustrated*, except it's all boys. All buff and beautiful . . ."

"In bathing suits, right?" I say.

"Yes, Willa." Tina rolls her eyes. Then she whispers to Ruby, "Well, most of them, anyway." She and Ruby laugh. "Just kidding."

"Who's going to publish it?" I ask.

"Oh, Willa," Ruby huffs, rolling her eyes. "You're such a Debbie Downer. Details, details. Leave it to you to worry about something."

Tina looks at me like she feels bad. "I haven't seen you around, Willa. Let's do something this weekend," she says.

"I'm busy," I say, and then I brighten up. "Guess what? I'm doing my first solo wedding on Saturday."

"Wow," Tina says. "Who?"

"Sam's sister."

"Your mother's letting you?" Ruby says. Ruby remembers how, when I first moved to Bramble, Ruby's aunt was getting married and my mother wouldn't let me near her wedding planning studio.

"Yes," I say. "Mom and I are partners now." I look at Tina. She smiles but doesn't seem excited. I think of how thrilled she was just a few short years ago when her favorite soap star was getting married and my mother was planning the wedding and Tina and I snuck into the reception. That seems like so long ago now.

"Let's go," Ruby says to Tina. "You know, Willa, so many lifeguards, so little time."

Tina looks at me, then turns to join Ruby.

I watch them walk away.

I stop by Nana's to pick up candy for Nico and Sofia, lots and lots of it, and bike over to visit them like I promised.

Mr. Sanchez is home today. He says he wants to

talk with my mother about a *quinceañera* party at the inn for Mariel when she turns fifteen in August.

"Papa, no," I hear Mare whisper, "You know we can't afford —" but he puts his hand up to silence her.

When I get home, my mother's coming in all red and sweating from jogging. "You're running late today," I say. She usually runs first thing in the morning.

"I'm starting to train for the Falmouth Road Race," she says. "It's always so hot, I want to get myself conditioned."

"How long is it again?" I ask.

"Ten-K . . . six point two miles," she says, turning to leave. She swings back around. "Hey, Willa, want to run it with me?"

I feel a surge of happiness. My mother hardly ever asks me to do anything with her. She's always so busy. "Uh, sure, maybe," I say. "If I can. I've never run more than three or four miles, but . . ."

"I'll write up a training program," Mom says, all happy. "You've got time. If you're serious, that is."

"Sure, yes," I say. "Count me in." I wonder whether Mom should be running so much so soon after losing the baby, but I'm sure she checked with her doctor. I wish I could ask if she and Sam are planning on trying again, but . . .

Mom grabs two water bottles from the fridge. She hands me one. I take it. "Thanks." This isn't the time to talk environmental issues, but maybe it's the time to talk about Salty. "Mom, I went to the shelter to visit the dog today."

She looks at me. Takes a long drink of water. Wipes sweat from her face. "And . . ."

"And the owners still haven't showed up."

"Well, I hope they do soon," she says, finishing her water. "Are you all set with everything for Sam's sister's wedding Saturday evening? I realize I've been so tied up with the Caldor event that I haven't even inquired."

"Thanks," I say. "I'm good. I went over the menu with Rosie and checked over the ceremony stuff with Sam. It's going to be in the Labyrinth, fingers crossed it doesn't rain. And I'm going to ask my friend Mariel if she'll . . ."

"Good," Mom says. "Sounds like you've thought of everything. I'm sorry, but I don't have time to . . ."

"I understand," I say. "On Saturday, you will be Wedding Planner one and I'll be Wedding Planner two."

Mom smiles at me, then looks at the clock. "Oh, gosh, look at the time. I've got to shower. Willa, please do a dining room check for me, will you? Make sure all the tables are set properly and that the girls used the new linens. Those old tablecloths were getting shabby."

Well, at least she didn't say "no" about adopting the dog again. I still have time to figure out a way to change her mind.

Up in my room, I go online and search under "water bottles." Tons of articles come up. I search "Planet Partners" and, lo and behold, there's a picture of the founder, Ruthie Gracemore. She looks like Sam's twin, only shorter and skinnier. The article talks about a new irrigation system they've just brought to three villages in Nicaragua. I search under the keywords "polluted Ganges River" and up come photos. One of a girl about my age. Her big brown eyes are bulging out of her face. Hollow-cheeked, she's just about to drink a skinny handful of water. *Don't do it.* I wish I could help her. I feel sad and hopeless, like, what can I do to help that girl, that particular girl right there in that photo. I wonder what her name is. I wonder how old she is. I wonder if she's gotten some fresh, clean water by now.

Water, water, everywhere. I think of that day on the beach, how thirsty I was, how awful it would be to be really thirsty, actually dying from thirst.

Maybe I will find a way to raise money for Planet Partners or for the organization Dr. Swaminathan is connected with in India. I think of Dr. Swammy's bumper sticker. THINK GLOBAL. START LOCAL.

Tonight I choose *Missing May* by Cynthia Rylant. I first read it when I was in fourth grade, one of those books you come back to again. It's so hopeful. And I like that the girl's name is Summer.

I write in my journal.

Only one more day until Ruthie arrives. Curious.
Only two more days until Joseph leaves. Sad.
Only three more days until my first solo wedding. Excited.
Only four more days until Salty is mine. Hoorah!

CHAPTER 17

Two Planets Colliding

There are persons both of superior character and intellect
Whose superiority quite disappears when they are put together.
They neutralize, anticipate, puzzle and belittle each other.
— Ralph Waldo Emerson

Mom and Sam are in the kitchen having coffee early Thursday morning before Rosie and the others arrive.

"Willa assures me she has everything under control for the wedding," Mom says. "Oh, and I'm putting them in the Norman Rockwell suite on the third floor."

"That's a very nice room," Sam says. "Thank you."

"And you said you think they have twelve or thirteen friends coming," Mom says. "I'm assuming they expect to stay here. I'm saving the Whitman Lodge by the pond."

"Great," Sam says, "thank you."

"I've got a luncheon today," Mom says, "the Caldor rehearsal tomorrow, and then Saturday, as you know, I'll be completely tied up all day with the wedding and reception. All I'll have time to do is shower and show up in the Labyrinth Saturday night at six."

"Stella . . ." Sam says. There's a long pause. "I appreciate your willingness to bend a bit on this one."

"What do you mean 'bend a bit'?" There's an edge to my mother's voice.

"I just mean that I know how you like to run things, and this was sprung upon you at the last minute and . . ."

"Sam, honey," Mom says. "She's your *sister*. I'll deal with it."

Way to go, Mom. I like the new bendable Stella. I think of that little green rubbery toy I had as a child. You could stretch and bend him every which way. What was that guy's name?

"Morning, Mom. Morning, Dad." I head to the corner area where we keep a small refrigerator, pantry, and bread box for our family's special food things. Rosie, Makita, Darryl, all of our employees, are welcome to have the meals we serve guests at the inn, but the stuff in this section is just for the family.

I open the bread box and reach for the two chocolate-cherry muffins I stashed there yesterday. They're gone. I check our refrigerator, the cabinets. I ask Mom and Sam. No, they haven't seen them.

"That's odd that you say that, Willa," Sam says.

"Yesterday I was looking for a block of cheddar cheese to make a sandwich. I could have sworn I just bought one. Oh, well, I'm headed up to take a shower. A nice, long shower. Maybe the last one I'll take in peace this week."

"What are you talking about?" Mom says.

"Oh, nothing," Sam says, winking at me, "just don't want to waste water."

When Sam leaves, the phone rings. Mom answers it. "Oh, yes, Ruthie, hello! This is Stella. Yes, me, too. You're where? Okay. I'll come pick you up. No, it's not a problem at all. I'll be there in a little over an hour. I'll come to the passenger pickup zone. I drive a silver SUV.

"Willa," Mom says. "I'm off to get your Aunt Ruthie and Spruce. They took an earlier flight. Don't tell Sam. Let's surprise him."

"Good for you, Mom."

"What?" she says, cocking her head suspiciously.

"Nothing. I mean that's nice of you."

When Sam comes downstairs, he says he'll be back in a bit and goes outside.

I look out the window and watch him walking slowly through his Labyrinth. When he reaches the center, he sits on the gray stone bench. He closes his eyes. I look away. This is Sam's special way of connecting with God. I leave him to his private prayers.

I go get my wedding planning book and bring it down to the kitchen table to look over the plans for Ruthie and Spruce's wedding. Ceremony, set. Reception . . . Sam will set up tables on the pavilion by the pond and I've ordered a tent just in case. Flowers . . . I have a feeling Ruthie will want simple, so I'm going to make her bouquet and the table centerpieces myself from the wildflowers on our property . . . daisies, cornflowers, thistles, and Queen Anne's lace. I love that name, *Queen Anne's lace.*

That reminds me of a funny story I read once about the origin of wedding customs. Back in the 1500s, most couples got married in June because they took their annual bath in May and still smelled pretty good by June. Just to be safe, though, brides carried a bouquet of flowers to hide body odor. And that's where the custom of a wedding bouquet comes from.

Dinner, set. I went over the menu with Rosie yesterday. She told me all of the ingredients she'll need and I made a shopping list.

Rosie will make the cake Saturday morning along with the Caldor cake, and I'll add the charms to each. For music, I hired "The Wedding Man." Mother gave me his card. She said he's not very original, but he's punctual and cheap. He brings a stock supply of dance songs and takes requests. I'm not sure what Ruthie and Spruce will want for their "first song," but Mr. Manny, aka The Wedding Man, says he's got pretty much anything they might ask for.

Oh, my gosh, I forgot to ask Mariel if she'll sing at the ceremony. Must do that first thing this morning.

When Sam comes in, he says he's off to get groceries.

"Oh, good," I say. "Can I come? I have a list for Ruthie's wedding dinner."

"Sure," Sam says. "I'd appreciate the company. Shopping's a lonely sport."

We drive to the Stop 'N Shop in Mashpee. It's early and the market is nearly empty. A few hours from now it will be packed. We each take a cart and split up. I've never shopped on my own before. This is fun. I start in the produce section since I have a lot of vegetables on my list. The tomatoes and basil are coming from Sam's garden, but I need garlic, shallots, asparagus, broccoli, red peppers, and avocadoes, lots of them. Rosie says avocado is the vegetarian's cheese.

The pasta is next. There's an organic foods section. I figure that's what Ruthie would want. I find a nice whole wheat pasta — linguine — and put several boxes in my cart. I choose a bottle of olive oil.

Next, French bread for the bruschetta. It smells so yummy in the bakery section. My stomach growls. I didn't have breakfast yet. I use the silver tongs to take two cinnamon Danish pastries from the display case, one for me and one for Sam, and pop them in a little white bag.

Sam and I meet up at the checkout counter. Sam's cart is full. We bag the groceries in the yellow plastic Stop 'N Shop bags. "Good thing we have two carts," Sam says. We eat the Danish on the way home.

Mother's car is in the side driveway. Sam will be so surprised.

"Now the unloading," Sam says. "I don't know

which I hate more, the shopping or the schlepping it home and unpacking."

I take two yellow shopping bags in each hand, the stuff that needs to be refrigerated, and Sam takes three bags in each hand, and we head into the kitchen.

Mother moves toward us like a storm cloud.

"She's a monster," Mother says. "Why didn't you tell me she's a nutcase? Do you know how much carbon dioxide an SUV emits each year? My hair's a rat's nest because the air conditioner was a 'senseless waste of energy' and so we had to drive with the windows down. I offered them a bottled water, thinking they might be thirsty from their trip, and you would have thought I was offering her hemlock." We hear footsteps coming. Mother looks toward the doorway and lowers her voice. "The nerve of her making me feel guilty in my own car, doing her a favor picking her and her tree man up from the airport . . ."

"Samuel!"

We turn and there's Aunt Ruthie. Short and skinny, with long, dark brown hair and Sam's big blue eyes.

Sam sets down the grocery bags.

She comes toward him. They hug briefly. She taps his tummy. "Chunking up a bit, are we? And this must be Willa, my wedding planner."

Mother huffs audibly.

"Hello, Aunt Ruthie. Nice to meet you." I attempt to hug her, but she shakes my hand instead.

"What's this, Sam," Ruthie says like a sergeant at boot camp. I swear Sam clicks his heels and stands taller at attention.

Ruthie waves her hands over our yellow grocery bags like she's discovered hidden enemy ammunition.

"Groceries," Sam says quietly.

Duh, I think. Isn't that obvious?

"*Sssch, ssssch, ssssch,*" Ruthie makes a loud disapproving clucking sound. "Sam, Sam, Sam . . . what in the good Goddess's name am I going to do with you? Where are your reusable hemp bags? Do you know how many millions of barrels of oil it takes to produce these awful, awful throwaway plastic bags? They end up on the bottom of oceans and lakes and kill the fish and . . ."

"*Excuse me,*" my mother says in her general's voice. She composes herself and smiles sweetly. "But we have groceries to put away and a breakfast to put on and so may I suggest that we continue this conversation later?"

I run outside to get the rest of those awful, awful bags. My mother and Ruthie are like two planets colliding.

There's a boy by the trunk of Sam's car. At first I think he's Jessie, from school, but no.

He looks at me for a brief second, then turns and runs.

Who the heck is that?

CHAPTER 18

Wave Talk

If the sea teaches any lesson,
It thunders this through the throat of all its winds.
"That there is no knowledge that is not valuable."
— Ralph Waldo Emerson

Sam says he's going to take Ruthie and Spruce on a little "sightseeing jaunt."

"Good, drop her off at the ferry dock in Hyannis and buy her a one-way trip to Nantucket," Mother whispers.

"Stella, I'm sorry," Sam says. "I should have warned you."

Sam leaves and I help Mother with last-minute things for the Caldor rehearsal dinner tomorrow night. The doorbell rings. It's Ruby's father, Mr. Sivler.

I hear him explaining to Mother how the Bramble Beach Association is filing a legal injunction against the Audubon Society, claiming the superiority of people and their pets over wild animals like the plovers.

He must be the person who wrote that awful message about serving the plovers piping hot with fries. I have half a mind to say something, but I have no proof.

Mr. Sivler asks Mom to sign a petition. He gives her a flag, #279. "Bring this with you when your family is at Sandy Beach," he says. "This is how we'll identify property owners."

"Does he think he owns the ocean, too?" I say to Mom after Mr. Sivler leaves. "And what's he doing, going door-to-door like that, running for mayor or something?"

Mom laughs. "He's the president of the Bramble Beach Association — the BBA is just trying to protect our rights."

"Well, I'm not using that flag," I say. "I think it's stupid. We don't own that sand. That beach was here a long time before we were, and those birds, well, I think we have an obligation to protect them. So what if people are a little inconvenienced."

"Now *you* sound like you're running for office," Mom says.

"Maybe I will," I say.

The Bramble Animal Shelter isn't open yet. I bike over to Mariel's to ask her if she'll sing at Ruthie's wedding.

"I'd be honored to, Willa," she says. "If I can. When is it?"

I give her the details about the music.

"I love 'Imagine,'" Mare says, smiling. "John Lennon. I sang it solo at my eighth-grade graduation. My momma was so proud." Her face brightens up. "Guess what? She may be coming home!"

"Oh, that's wonderful, Mare."

"Daddy is determined to have a *quinceañera* for me and Momma says she wouldn't miss it for the world."

"I'll look forward to meeting her." I'm looking at my friend's face, so happy. I'm smiling, but inside I'm thinking her mother just better not let her down.

I bike past the Bramble Library, then decide to pedal back and stop in.

Mrs. Saperstone is in the children's department staring out at the whale spoutin' fountain.

"Willa, hello! Come see the new benches and wildflower garden we've added out in the courtyard."

We walk outside. It's nice here. "How did your talk go the other night?" I ask.

"Went well, I think," she says with a smile. "The group of ladies staying at your inn certainly seemed to enjoy themselves."

"The Red Hats," I say. "They're fun."

"Yes, they are," Mrs. S says. "I'm going to get one of those hats, maybe start a Bramble chapter."

"Did Dr. Swaminathan come to your talk?" I ask, picking up a penny from the ground and casually tossing it into the fountain.

Mrs. Saperstone laughs. "You are such a sweet girl."

"What?" I say innocently. "What?"

"You don't fool me, Willa Havisham. Don't you think I realize who set Javid up to coming? All dressed in a smart summer poplin striped suit, with a box of my favorite chocolate cranberries, no less."

So, Dr. Swaminathan's first name is Javid. "Listen," I say, "if you need a good wedding planner, give me a call. I don't have business cards yet, but you know how to reach me."

"*Willa*," Mrs. Saperstone says in a shocked voice,

looking around, laughing. "We're a long way from the altar, but it sure is fun to be dating again."

Next, I go for a quick ride to the beach. A day I don't see the water is like a day I don't read. Every day it's different. Every day I learn something new.

It's high tide and the waves are sweeping powerfully onto shore. I listen as they talk to me. *Things are changing, things are changing, pay attention, pay attention.* I have an odd feeling something major is about to happen in my life.

When I get home, Sam is pulling into the parking lot. Aunt Ruthie gets out first. Sam introduces me to Spruce. He doesn't look like a pine tree at all. He's a tall, thin, handsome man, Asian, with dark, thoughtful eyes and a kind smile.

"Nice to meet you, Willa," he says, reaching out to shake my hand. "Thank you for planning our wedding. Ruth and I appreciate your efforts."

"My pleasure," I say. "I hope you'll be happy."

"Happy would be nice," Spruce says quietly.

"No, Ruthie," I hear Sam saying, sighing loudly like he's got a headache, which I imagine he probably does. "I don't know what my carbon footprint is. Or Stella's, either. But I think she wears a size seven shoe."

"Not funny, Samuel," Ruthie says. "I've just found the first way we can trade. Let me go get my questionnaire upstairs and I'll start carbon emission calculations on this household. It's nothing short of global ignorance not to know the extent of the damage you are doing to this planet, Samuel."

I look at Spruce. He looks uncomfortable and his eyebrows are scrunched like he wishes Ruthie would be quiet.

"Right off the bat," Ruthie says, "there's a huge problem with having two large truck-size vehicles in one tiny family of three. Haven't you heard of carpooling? Public transportation?"

I'm thinking Ruthie ought to be grateful that my mother drove all the way to Boston to pick her up this morning, but I keep my mouth closed.

Good time to get away. I bike over to visit Salty Dog. He licks my face, all happy to see me.

Mr. Sweeney says, "Good news, still no owner, yet."

Thank you, thank you.

Now I just need to find a way to convince Stella to let me adopt him. Maybe if I offered to work extra shifts all summer. No, I already do my fair share for our family. Or, maybe I could promise to keep Salty in my room and train him to stay away from the living room and dining room and all the good furniture. No, I have a feeling that dog has a mind of his own, used to roaming the wide open beach like he owns it. I doubt I'd be able to restrict him like that.

I stop by Sweet Bramble Books. Both sides of the store are packed with tourists. *Good!* There's a new endcap of *Edward's Eyes* by Patricia MacLachlan. I loved her book *Sarah, Plain and Tall*. On the back jacket of the book is a photo of the author hugging a dog. The flap copy mentions Cape Cod. It's a skinny book. I have Dr. Swaminathan ring it up for me with our family discount. I'm about to mention Mrs. Saperstone when Nana calls me from the candy side.

"Willa," she says. "Come see! I started wrapping the taffy in tags last night and already people are noticing. And I had an idea of my own. I set up a little suggestion box and listen to this. Some boy gave us a good one." She holds up a paper to read:

Don't be daffy. Eat your taffy.

"He was very handsome, had a British accent. I thought about you, but . . ."

"I have a boyfriend, Nana."

"I know, I know," she says.

When I get home, I go to look for Aunt Ruthie.

She's standing outside facing the Labyrinth.

"Hi, Aunt Ruthie," I say. "Do you have a few minutes to go over the wedding plans?"

She turns to me. She's crying.

"What's wrong?" I ask.

"I don't know if I can go through with this." She lets out a sob, then turns and runs into the inn.

Life sure is full of surprises.

CHAPTER 19

Kindred Spirits After All

To believe your own thought,
to believe that what is true for you in your private heart
is true for all men — that is genius.
— Ralph Waldo Emerson

I'm not sure how, but I want to help Aunt Ruthie. Spruce seems nice, but I don't feel comfortable breaking the news to him that his fiancée may not want to get married!

Sam is in his study writing. When he sees me in the doorway, he slides the yellow tablet into his desk. I tell him about Ruthie crying. Sam says he isn't quite sure what to do. "I wish my mother was still alive," he says.

Rosie shrugs her shoulders when I tell her. "I think you need to leave her alone, Willa," Rosie says, "give her some space. Everyone gets emotional before weddings."

Given how busy Mom is and given how she and Ruthie seem to despise each other, I approach my mother as a last resort. When I tell her what happened, she looks at me for a moment and then her eyes begin to glisten. She smiles and says, "Don't worry, Willa. I'll talk to her."

What? I'm amazed. "Thank you, Mom," I say.

JFK calls to say he's leaving today. A day early! He's coming over at four to say good-bye.

I start crying as soon as I get off the phone. I don't want him to go.

It's good that I'm getting the tears out now, though. I don't want our last time together to be sad. *Stupid baseball.* I glance at the cover of *Edward's Eyes*. There's a boy holding a baseball glove, looking so happy. I start reading. I'm finished in an hour. It's a beautiful story. JFK would like it.

I make a quick trip to Cohen's card shop and I'm waiting on the porch with a gift bag when JFK arrives. A cry catches in my throat, but I push it back down and smile a happy smile for him. He's carrying a paper bag with a shiny red holiday bow stuck on. "For you," he says.

It's a reusable water bottle just like his.

"You said you wanted green, right?"

"Yes," I say, laughing. "Thank you."

"I know it's not the kind of present girls like," he says.

"It's perfect," I say, "I'll start using it today. And besides, you already gave me the perfect present." I show him the silver locket I wear every day.

"Still got my picture in there?" he says.

"Maybe," I say, then laugh. "And here, this is for you." I hand him the bag.

He unwraps the pocket-size, black-lined journal — Moleskine, it's called. Hemingway loved these. "To catch your lyric ideas," I say. The other gift is *Edward's Eyes*. "It's about baseball and something more."

He smiles. I hug him.

We go to Bloomin' Jean's for ice cream. JFK promises to call. I tell him to have a great time in Florida. "See ya in August," he says.

Be brave, Willa, be brave. It's only for a month.

Mom says she had a good talk with Ruthie. She doesn't tell me details, just that Ruthie is a "very strong-willed and independent woman," used to only focusing on herself and her work, and she was getting last-minute cold feet about sharing her life with someone else. She loves Spruce very much. It's just that she loves her work, too.

"I could relate," Mom says.

I smile at my mother. "Nothing wrong with being strong-willed, independent, and happily married, too," I say. "There's a way to be queen and not kill the king."

Mom bursts out laughing and hugs me. "Who raised you to be so smart?" she says.

"Seems to me you and Aunt Ruthie are kindred spirits after all."

"Maybe," Mom says, "but I'm not about to stop blow-drying my hair."

We laugh. "Mom . . . about the dog."

Her happy face hardens. "Please, Willa, stop. I'm sorry to disappoint you, but this isn't the time to bring home a dog."

"When is the right time?"

"I don't know, Willa. It's something we would need to talk about and plan for. We just finished furnishing the inn and everything is just the way I like it."

"But, Mom, I really, really want this dog. I love this dog."

She sighs. "Willa, it's a stray. It could be sick or —"

"He's fine, Mother. I've been visiting him every day and he's healthy and —"

"You've been visiting him every day? Oh, Willa. What am I going to do with you?"

"Let me adopt Salty?"

"*Salty?*" Mother starts to say something, then stops. "Willa, I'm sorry. I've got to meet with the bandleader for the Caldor reception. I'll think about —"

"Oh, Mom, thank you," I hug her tight.

"Wait, Willa. I'm not promising anything."

"I know. I know. Just, thank you!"

I run to my room and call Mariel.

She laughs and I hear Sofia and Nico laughing in the background, too. "Why are you so surprised, Willa? I told you. That dog belongs to you."

I'm so happy I could burst. Just a few more days and Salty's coming home!

Later, Mom knocks on my door. "Willa, you wanted to come to the staff meeting, right?"

Mother has name tags and a marker so that we can

all learn one another's names. I listen respectfully as Mother, and then Sam, discuss their lists of issues. When the time is right, I ask if I may make a suggestion.

"Certainly," Mom says. Sam nods encouragingly.

"I think we should adopt a no-water-bottle policy here at the inn." I share the statistics JFK gave me about throwaway plastic water bottles and the information I learned from the Internet and the heartbreaking story about polluted water that Dr. Swaminathan shared with me.

Sam shakes his head. "Good idea, Willa. There are a lot of other things we can do like that. I'll purchase reusable grocery shopping bags the next time I go."

Darryl says, "I've been wanting to suggest that we offer guests the option of reusing towels and bed linens, rather than washing all those towels and sheets every day. We waste so much water and energy."

"I like that idea," I say. "I could write up little cards for the room explaining that we're trying to be more earth-friendly here at the Bramblebriar."

A few other people make suggestions. Mother seems to be agreeable. This is good. We're starting small, but who knows where this will lead. I think of Dr. Swammy's bumper sticker, THINK GLOBAL. START

LOCAL. I feel proud that the Bramblebriar is going greener.

Someone coughs and I turn around. Aunt Ruthie is standing in the doorway with her arms folded, nodding her head, smiling. I bet she thinks she inspired all of this. Well, that's fine by me.

CHAPTER 20

Willa the Wedding Planner

The reward of a thing well done,
is to have done it.

— Ralph Waldo Emerson

Saturday morning dawns bright and beautiful. Rosie finishes the two wedding cakes and I carefully add the wishing well charms. Mother is bustling about in top form, barking orders at everyone about the Caldor reception before heading off to Bramble United Community for the ceremony. I wonder who the new minister will be tomorrow?

Sam is mowing the walkway in the Labyrinth. The puffy blue hydrangea, sweet-smelling red-and-pink dianthus, the roses, and all the wildflowers, too, are flaunting their petals like bridesmaid dresses swooshing back and forth on the dance floor.

I look up. Not a cloud in the sky. No need for a tent tonight.

Ruthie and Spruce's guests arrive and I escort them to the Lodge. I talk with their friend, Michael, about the service. I explain to Ruthie and Spruce how the ceremony will go, the two of them, walking one, then the other, through the circle path of the Labyrinth to the stone bench in the center where their guests and Sam and Mom and I will be waiting. Ruthie and Spruce asked Sam and Mom to be best man and maid of honor.

I see that the tables are set up on the pavilion, twinkle lights strung around the borders. I pick daisies and brown-eyed Susans and Queen Anne's lace and arrange them in simple vases for centerpieces. I make a hydrangea bouquet for Ruthie and set it in water in a cool place in the kitchen. I double-check the menu with Rosie and leave notes for the staff members working tonight. I call the DJ. He's all set.

Then I remember something. All those years when Mother wouldn't let me help with the weddings, I had a little secret ritual. Mother was known for her signature Twelve Perfect Ingredients for a happy wedding day. I would sneak down to her studio the night before the weddings and add a little ingredient of my own. I would sew a cherry pit into the hems of the wedding gowns. Just a symbol, really. A little seed of good luck and a reminder that the work of a happy marriage was just beginning. After the glow of the Cinderella ball, the perfect gown and food and music and flowers, from that day forward, it's all about the love.

Quickly, I bike to Nana's store. Good thing she has cherry cordials in the case. When I get home, I offer to press Aunt Ruthie's wedding dress and she agrees. I take it to my room and carefully, very carefully, sew in the Willa Havisham Thirteenth Secret Ingredient. I close my eyes and make a wish for Aunt Ruthie and Spruce. "And PS, it would be nice to have some cousins."

It's going to be a beautiful wedding.

Oh, no, a *photographer.*

I completely forgot! Who can I get on such short notice?

A car passing by catches my eye and I look across the yard to No Mutts About It. There are bunches of gold and silver helium balloons waving in the breeze and a large banner above the door, GRAND OPENING TODAY. I run over.

Ruby and Tina are serving punch in the lobby. There are two silver-tiered serving trays with dog-bone-shaped cookies, one marked "Poochies," the other marked "Parents."

"Willa," Ruby says, "welcome." She scoops me a ladle of punch.

"Guess what," Tina says. "No, you tell her, Rube, it's your story."

"This place is haunted," Ruby whispers, smiling sweetly at a lady with a tiny pinch-faced dog. "Hello, Mrs. Fieldstone. Hello, Fe-Fe. Such a pretty girl!"

"The workers couldn't get the door open on one of the upstairs rooms," Ruby says. "It was barricaded somehow from inside. Finally, they had to break the door down. And, guess what? Someone was living there!"

So that explains the movement at the window.

There's a commotion behind us. "Darling!" Mrs. Sivler says, moving toward the doorway to hug a lady with two tall Dalmatian dogs. "Welcome to No Mutts About It."

"Ruby," I say. "I have a favor to ask you."

"Sure, Willa, what?"

I tell her about the wedding and ask if she'd be willing to be our photographer. "I saw what a great job you're doing with the lifeguards. I'm sorry for the short notice, but it's my first solo wedding and somehow I forgot about pictures."

"Oh, that's right," Tina shouts. "It's your wedding planning debut! Congratulations, Willa. I'm so proud of you. I want to come see. Can I come, too?"

"Sure," I say, "that would be great."

This day couldn't be turning out better. I race to the shelter to see Salty.

Mr. Sweeney looks up when I come in the door. I can tell by his face, something's wrong.

"I'm sorry, Willa," he says. "The dog's owner came early this morning. He had the paperwork and tags and everything."

"No," I say, slumping down in a chair, my heart rushing up to my throat like I'm choking. "Who are they? What took them so long? If they loved that dog, they would have claimed him before now."

"I'm sorry, Willa. I really hoped it would work out for you. But the owner is a very nice boy, a few years older than you, I'd say. He's not from around here. Sounded British to me. He was visiting friends on Martha's Vineyard and rode his boat over. He had it harbored out off the Spit and the dog jumped overboard."

Mr. Sweeney talks some more, mentions other nice dogs and cats who would make "lovely pets," but there is no substitute for Salty. I love that dog.

He was mine.

Heading back to the inn, I'm in no mood for a wedding. But this is Ruthie's day and I'm her wedding planner, so I push my sad feelings down deep inside and lock them up tight till later.

The inn is packed when I get home. My mother is waiting for me. The Caldor ceremony went smoothly and now the reception is well under way. My mother looks gorgeous in a pale blue linen suit. "Willa," she says, "I've been thinking. And talking with Sam. I've decided to let you adopt that dog."

A sob slips out and I dash upstairs before I scare all the cheerful wedding guests.

Ruthie and Spruce's wedding is perfect. The Labyrinth feels holy and magical. Mariel sings like an angel. The bride and groom hold hands and face each other and speak their vows eyes to eyes as if they are the only two people here. But we are here, to witness their obvious, deep love for each other. Ruthie and Spruce cry. Mom and Sam cry. I look over and catch Tina's eye. She puts her hands together as if she is clapping for me and then gives me a thumbs-up sign. I hold my composure. I am a professional, after all.

The dinner is delicious. The Wedding Man takes requests and because the party is small, everyone gets one of the wedding cake charms. Each corresponds to a letter in the name of our inn:

B . . . a book

R . . . a rose

A . . . an angel

M . . . a mirror

B . . . a beach dune

L . . . a labyrinth

E . . . an envelope

B . . . a butterfly

R . . . a ring

I . . . an inkwell

A . . . an anchor

R . . . a rainbow

I let all the guests go ahead of me. There is one ribbon left.

The inkwell. I hold the little charm in my hand and smile.

"What one did you get?" my mother asks.

I show her. "That's right," she says. "My daughter, the writer."

My eyes fill up.

"I'm so sorry about the dog," she says.

"I know, Mom. Let's not talk about it right now."

"Sure," she says, "I understand." A song pumps up, an oldie about girls just wanting to have fun. "Come on," she says, "let's dance."

And for the first time ever, I dance with my mother.

She's a decent dancer for a mother.

CHAPTER 21

A Startling Surprise on the Spit

I wish the days to be as centuries,
loaded, fragrant.

— Ralph Waldo Emerson

Surprise, surprise. Guess who gave the sermon at BUC this morning?

Sam. My wonderful father, the poet, writer, and most of all, great teacher, Sam Gracemore. Nana explained that while the BUC Board of Directors is searching for a new minister, they've asked certain members of the congregation to give the sermons. They are supposed to talk about their spiritual journey, what they "believe."

Sam talks about how he was raised in "the Unitarian Universalist tradition" and like two of the early leaders of this faith, Ralph Waldo Emerson and Henry

Thoreau, he finds his greatest connection to God in nature, and like Emerson, he believes in making time for solitude, for being totally quiet and alone so as to listen to the voice within.

"Emerson said he believed that what was true in his heart was true for others as well." Sam looks down at me from the pulpit and smiles. He continues talking. I look around the room. Everyone is paying attention. *I'm so proud of you, Dad.* I give him a little thumbs-up sign that only he can see, and he smiles at me and winks.

"In conclusion . . . I believe we are all connected . . . people, plants, animals. I believe that in our search for the divine, we need look no further than the sound of the mourning dove, or the scent of the wild beach rose. We need look no further than into the eyes of the one seated next to us."

I look at my mother and her eyes are brimming, too.

After brunch, I change into comfortable clothes. I can't wait to get to the beach.

I rush down the stairs, flip off my sandals, and set

off toward the Spit like I'm already prepping for the Falmouth Road Race. Mom says official training starts tomorrow.

The beach is fairly empty. They forecasted rain. I keep running, the sand cool and soft beneath my feet.

Out at the end, the endangered bird sign has been repainted. The ropes are intact. A tern scampers fast in front of me, leaving little three-pronged prints in his wake. There's a boat anchored and someone is sitting on the sand. As I get closer, I see it's a boy, older than me.

He turns to me and smiles. He looks sixteen, maybe seventeen, blue eyes, very handsome. He looks familiar, but I'm not sure why. He holds up the book he's reading and smiles. "Read any David Almond? The man is bloody brilliant."

How do I know this boy? Then it dawns on me. "You were at the inn, by my father's car the other day. When I saw you, you ran."

"And I saw you yesterday," the boy says. "All dollied up fancy, dancing."

My heart starts pounding. "Where were you?"

"I've been observin' you this past week, but I had to clear out yesterday when the mutt place opened."

"That was you up in the window?" Now I'm scared. "Why were you watching me?"

"To see if you were worth traveling all this way to find," he says, laughing. "You used to live in a *funeral home*? That's bloody creepy, don't you think?"

"What's creepy is you spying on me . . ."

I hear barking and then there he is . . . My dog!

Salty bounds over the dune and runs to me. I bend down and he lick, lick, licks my face. Then he turns and bolts over to the boy.

"There's my dog," the boy says, laughing, ruffling the dog's furry head. "There's my Salty Dog."

"How do you know his name?" I say.

"Ought to know my own dog's name, don't you think?"

"*His name is really Salty?*" I say, incredulous.

"I just told you that, didn't I? I finally found him yesterday. When we came ashore last Saturday, this lady said no dogs allowed on the beach. I told her to bug off. She said I had to go or she'd call the coppers. Something about birds called the piping plovers. I said my mum would serve 'em up hot with bangers. The lady said, 'What's bangers?' and I explained. She said, 'You're in America now, son. We call them French fries here.'"

"So, it was you who put that paper on my Bramble Board."

"Figured you could use something more lively,"

he says. "Those candy floss poems'll put ya to sleep, Willa."

How does he know my name? "How do you know my . . ."

"Willa!"

I turn. JFK is walking toward me.

"I thought you'd left!" I say.

JFK looks past me to the boy with the dog. "My flight was overbooked," he says, "then I had to go somewhere with my dad. I'm not leaving till tonight. Your mom said you'd be here."

JFK looks at me and then at the boy. They stare at each other for a second. "Who are you?" JFK asks in a suspicious-sounding voice. JFK puffs out his chest and stands taller. I can't believe it, but he's jealous. He looks even cuter when he's jealous.

Here I am on the beach with two beautiful boys. Ooooh . . . this is sort of fun.

"Don't worry, bloke," the boy says to JFK. "I'm not her boyfriend. I'm her brother."

TO BE CONTINUED

Willa's Summer Skinny-Punch Pix List

Bronx Masquerade, Nikki Grimes
Edward's Eyes, Patricia MacLachlan
Esperanza Rising, Pam Muñoz Ryan
Green Angel, Alice Hoffman
The Hundred Dresses, Eleanor Estes
Locomotion, Jacqueline Woodson
Love That Dog, Sharon Creech
Missing May, Cynthia Rylant
True Believer, Virginia Euwer Wolff
The Whipping Boy, Sid Fleischman

Dear Reader,

What books would you add? Maybe you'd like to start your own Pix List.

Happy Reading,
☺ Colleen

_____ 's

Pix List

_____

_____

_____

_____

_____

_____

_____

_____

_____

_____

_____

Acknowledgments

With sincerest thanks to: my wonderful Scholastic Press editor, Jennifer Rees, for her excellent questions, suggestions, and generous use of smiley faces; David Levithan and all of Willa's friends at Scholastic Book Clubs and Fairs; my dear UK Macmillan editor, Ruth Alltimes, who cheers Willa on from "across the pond"; my agents, Tracey and Josh Adams; all of the librarians, teachers, and booksellers who introduce readers to my books; my mother, Peg Spain Murtagh; my sons, Christopher, Connor, and Dylan; and, most especially, my loyal fans who have grown to love Willa and JFK, Stella and Sam, Nana, Mum, Tina, Ruby, Mariel, and the seaside town of Bramble, Cape Cod. Many of you have written to say that Willa is inspiring you to read the books on her "Willa's Pix" lists, to start keeping journals, and to write stories of your own. Whoo-hoo! That makes me (and Willa) so happy.

Read on. Write on. Dream BIG.

Till soon,
☺ Colleen

About the Author

Coleen Murtagh Paratore is the author of the popular The Wedding Planner's Daughter series as well as *The Funeral Director's Son, Mack McGinn's Big Win, Sunny Holiday,* and several picture books. The mother of three teenage sons, she lives in upstate New York and on Cape Cod, Massachusetts. Visit Coleen online at www.coleenparatore.com.